Sympathetic Magic

by

Sara Bourgeois

D1528061

Chapter One

It was a dark and stormy night.

Just kidding...

It was actually a boiling hot afternoon. The kind where you walk outside, and it feels like you just walked into an armpit. Humid, and air so thick it's like walking through soup. Those analogies are gross together, but I could only hope it painted a picture of what we were dealing with in Coventry.

The Skeenbauer Coven could have used some magic to make the clouds roll in to block out some of the sun or just summoned a breeze, but I was the new leader. I'd decided that it was in all of our best interests to only use magic when we really needed it.

It wasn't a law per se. We weren't putting people in a jar for using magic to clean their houses or make their banana bread taste a little better, but it was a strong suggestion.

Anyway, it was hot.

And it was staying that way.

Reggie spent the night at Hangman's House with me because the air conditioning in her little crackerbox house had gone out again. And by again, it was the third time in a week. She'd scraped together the money to fix it the first two times, and it had gone out again the very next day. She couldn't afford to have the HVAC guy come out again for an emergency call, so I'd let her crash at my place.

"We'll go over there after work, and I'll fix it," I said. "And next time, just call me. You don't need to pay repairmen."

"But your rules," she protested.

"Reggie, do you know what the low temperature was last night?"

"No..."

"It was eighty-five degrees. That's the coolest it got last night. I'd say that fixing your air conditioning isn't a frivolous use of magic. Plus, you spent all your savings, didn't you?"

"Yes, but…"

"No but, Reggie. You were going to use that money to buy a new car. When you got a more reliable car, you were going to be able to take your Grandma out of the nursing home for day trips."

"I was," she said.

"Well, now you're just going to have to use my car on the weekends until you get money saved up again," I said. "And after work today, we're going to your house to repair the air conditioning."

"Thank you," she said. "I miss having Jeremy in town to fix these things."

Jeremy Corey was one of Thorn's deputies, but he was also in the National Guard. He was normally only gone one weekend a month and a couple of weeks during the summer, but that spring he'd been called up for a mission in the Ukraine. Six weeks before he left the country, he'd been in Washington DC doing some sort of specialized training, and then they'd shipped him overseas.

Normally, Reggie didn't need my magic because if anything went wrong, she'd call up Jeremy, and he'd come running. With him out of town, she had a lot more free time in addition to her unmet repair needs.

"What would you like for breakfast?" I asked as she emerged from the guest bedroom.

She'd left the door open a crack so we could talk while she got dressed. "Oh, are you cooking?"

"Yes, we've got time. I'll make some coffee too, but don't worry, we'll still drop by the Brew Station and grab lattes before we open."

I'd moved the opening of the store to an hour later. We'd been opening up before the first ghost tour got done, but there'd been no point. No one came into my shop until that first tour ended. Sometimes it was even later than that because they'd go over to the Brew Station and grab a drink before wandering back over to buy souvenirs or pick up something from my selection of authentic magical tools.

"Oh, I get breakfast and a latte. Maybe my luck is changing," she said with a smile.

Unfortunately, she somehow managed to drop her purse, get her ankle caught up in the strap, and fall face first onto the hallway floor as she came out of the bedroom.

Reggie let out a chilling cry of pain, and when she pushed herself up from the floor with her palms, her nose was bleeding.

"Oh, gawd, I think I broke my nose. It hurts so bad," she said as her hand fluttered up to her face. Reggie flinched and quickly pulled it away as she got up onto her knees.

I immediately knelt beside her and covered her nose with my palm. She halfway recoiled away, but I felt all of the tension leave her as I healed the injury.

"What was that?" Meri asked as he came skittering up the stairs.

He was so tiny that he almost missed the landing. I suppressed a chuckle at the sight of him struggling to make the last step, but I didn't hide it fast enough. He narrowed his eyes at me.

"I thought maybe someone had let an elephant in the house and it died," he snarked.

"Meri, that's mean," I said. "Reggie fell and broke her nose."

But Reggie was laughing. "I'm fine, thank you," she said and stood up. "But really, thank you, Kinsley. I can't believe how much that hurt. If not for you, I'd have spent the morning in the emergency room in agony waiting to be seen."

"Well, we've got no time for that," I said. "Still feel like breakfast?"

"Of course," she said. "How about maple sausage and cheddar biscuits?"

"Deal, but only if you promise to use the railing when you go down the stairs."

"I feel like you're being a smart... aleck, but it's good advice. So, I'll follow its" she retorted with a grin.

I wasn't sure if I should go down the stairs before her to catch her if she fell or behind her so I could grab her if she took a tumble. I had no reason to believe Reggie would fall again, but for some reason, I was worried about her. Seeing her bleeding and in pain had shaken me up. I felt like a mother hen clucking over her chicks.

"What can I do to help?" Reggie asked once we were in the kitchen. "You know, I did help cook sometimes at the diner. I'm not totally incompetent in the kitchen."

"Then why are you always letting me cook for you?" I playfully wagged my finger in her direction.

She smiled mischievously. "Because you always offer."

"Okay, then. Why don't you do the sausage. You can add the maple and the spices to the ground pork while I work on the biscuit dough."

"Sounds simple enough,," Reggie said.

But apparently it wasn't simple at all. When she got into the cabinet to get the spices, she knocked half of them off the shelf. The cayenne pepper broke open and spilled everywhere. There was a cloud of the red spice in the air. It burned our eyes and made us cough.

I waved my hand in the air, and it quickly found its way back into the container. "Why don't you just keep me company," I said. "I'll just use a little magic to make this go faster."

Reggie tripped again on the way to the table but caught herself on the counter. "Oops," she said and then apologized to the chair when she kicked the leg.

"Are you all right?" I asked.

"Yeah. I just seem to be clumsy which is not something I've ever been. You can't be a clumsy waitress. Maybe I'm having a run of bad luck. Is that a thing?"

It was then I consciously noticed what had probably made me worry about Reggie earlier. She had sort of a dark aura around her. My subconscious had most likely picked up on it upstairs after she fell, but it had gotten darker. I doubted it was visible to anyone but me, but I could see it.

"Have you been in a bad mood lately?" I asked as I kneaded the dough.

"Not really. I was super sad when Jeremy left for a few months, but I've been feeling better about that lately."

"And right now, you don't feel sad or angry? Nothing like that?"

"No, why? What aren't you telling me?"

"Nothing," I said because I really wasn't sure what I was seeing, and I didn't want to freak her out until I knew.

"Stop lying to me this instant, Kinsley Skeenbauer. I can see right through you. When you lie to me, I can smell it like a fart in a car."

"Nice analogy," I said.

"Don't try and deflect. Tell me what you see."

"You have a dark aura," Meri said as his little booty sashayed into the room. "You're surrounded by black energy, but my guess is that Kinsley doesn't know why."

"Do you know why?" I asked Meri. "Because if you do, you should tell us."

"I would tell you if I did know, but I do not. I can tell you that whatever it is, it's not coming from inside her. It's wrapped around her. Like bubble wrap. Only not fun bubble wrap you can pop. It's more like bubble wrap of doom."

"So, it's a curse," I said.

"Or it's demonic oppression," Meri said casually.

Reggie's face blanched.

"Well, if it's demonic, then get rid of it," I said to Meri.

"You want me to blow her up?" he asked and sat down. "'Cause I can do that."

"No!" Reggie and I both exclaimed at the same time.

"Absolutely not," I said. "Isn't there anything else you can do besides blow her up?"

"Fine," he said with a sigh. "Let me give it a shot."

"Is he going to blow me up?" Reggie asked nervously.

"No. He's not," I said. "He's not going to blow you up."

Meri stood up and walked over to the table. After jumping up into the middle of it, he sat down and stared at Reggie. He let out a loud meow and then began to purr like an engine.

"That feels weird," Reggie said. "It feels like ants crawling under my skin."

"Hush," Meri said as Reggie began to squirm and scratch at her neck and arms. "And sit still."

"I'm trying," she said.

This went on for another minute or so until Meri jumped down off the table. "Not demonic," he said as he started to saunter out of the room.

"Then what is it?" I asked.

"I don't know. All I know is it's not demonic. I could blow her up anyway. It would solve the problem."

"No, thank you," I said through clenched teeth. "That won't be necessary."

"Let me know if you change your mind."

"We'll just eat breakfast, and then once we get into the shop, I'll try to discern what it is. It can't be that hard to get rid of, Reggie. I promise. I'm, like, the strongest witch in the world or something. I can fix this."

Halfway to the shop, my car broke down. I tried to use magic to get it started again, but it was dead.

"You can't fix it?" Reggie asked.

"Apparently not," I said.

"It's a brand new car. It can't just be dead."

I'd recently traded my ancient Subaru in for a new electric Volkswagen Microbus. Electric cars were the thing, and it was time for me to get on board with it. There were actually only two pumps left at the gas station at that point, and the rest were electric charging stations.

"It shouldn't be," I said. "And even if it was, I should be able to bring it back."

"You're trying to necromancy your car," Reggie said with a chuckle.

"Well, I'm glad you've got a sense of humor about this," I said.

"Are you mad at me?"

"Not at all. I really am glad you're taking this well," I said.

"But I killed your car. Your really cool new car."

"I'm sure it will be fine," I said. "I'll put in for a self-driving tow truck to bring it to the shop. Once we get you fixed up, I'm sure the Microbus will come roaring back to life."

Her comments about necromancy made my heart ache in a way I hadn't expected. I just hoped Reggie hadn't seen it written across my face.

I love your darkness.

It figured that Azriel would say something like that and then completely disappear. At least it had made things less complicated.

There was a part of me that was still chaotic and could, if I wanted to, control the shadow things. I knew that it called out to him, but he never answered. That made it easier for me to just enjoy my relationship with Thorn. It wasn't like I was torn between the two of them. I couldn't be. Azriel was gone.

That's what I'd wanted, right?

"So, we're walking then?" Reggie asked.

"It's not that far," I said. "I think it's actually the easiest option right now."

It only took us around ten minutes to walk to the Brew Station. We didn't have a car, but we were still stopping for coffee.

"You guys look a little... sweaty,," Viv said as we approached the counter.

It was true. While it was still fairly early in the morning, it was already hot outside. Reggie and I both had our hair half-plastered to our heads.

"The car broke down and we had to walk about halfway from my house," I said.

"You drove in together?" Viv asked.

"Yeah, my air conditioner is out again, so I crashed at Kinsley's place last night," Reggie said.

"Again?" Viv asked. "You should totally sue that guy who keeps charging you for emergency visits. He's obviously not fixing the issue."

I wanted to agree with her, but given what I knew about Reggie's current state, I knew it wasn't the guy's fault. She was breaking everything she touched.

13

"Well, we're going to figure out something else after work. We're not going to call him again," I said and gave her a wink.

"Oooh! Right," Viv said with a smile. "Gotcha."

"Dagnabbit!" Hank said.

That was followed by the sound of a metal container hitting the floor. We all looked in his direction and found one of Viv's espresso machines spewing steam.

"Oh, no," Reggie said.

"Hurry, Hank. Unplug that thing!"

"I'm just going to wait outside," Reggie said before rushing out the door.

"Wait, is she..," Viv started to ask.

"I'll tell you all about it later, I swear," I said. "For now can we get a large hazelnut iced coffee and a large iced chai latte?"

"Hank, will you get those drinks? I'm going to see about that espresso machine. I can't be down one today. Tourists are going to flock in here to get out of the heat."

"It's fixed," I said and waved my hand past it casually. "Give it a shot. I'm sure it's fine."

Hank ignored what I said, because that's what people in Coventry did, and went about making our drinks. Viv plugged her espresso machine back in and gave it a try.

"Well, I'll be... thanks!" Viv said.

"No, problem," I said. "I mean, you're welcome."

Hank handed me my drinks and Viv said, "On the house, hon. I hope your day gets better."

"Thanks. Thank you so much."

"Call me later?"

"You know it."

I walked out of the Brew Station and spotted Reggie sitting on one of the benches in the square. A bird nearly pooped on her, but I used just a touch of magic to divert it. The dark aura around her had already grown stronger too.

"Here's your coffee," I said making sure she had a tight grip on the plastic cup before I let go. "I got the iced versions."

"Thank you," she said and took a long draw from the straw. "It's good."

"You ready to head into work?" I asked.

"Am I going to die?" Reggie responded.

"What? No," I said.

"Because I almost got hit by a car walking over here. I had plenty of time, but the woman driving stomped on the accelerator. You should have seen her face. She was just as stunned and confused as I was."

"I'm not going to let that happen, Reggie. I promise."

We were nearly as protected inside the shop as we were at Hangman's House, so I left Reggie to run the cash register and help customers at the front counter while I gathered what I needed.

At worst, I thought, she might hurt herself, so I told her to stay behind the counter. A few people meandered in after a ghost tour, and I kept an eye on her while I grabbed candles, herbs, and a few crystals from the shelves.

Once I had everything I needed, I went into the back room and closed the door. I had to act quickly because I wasn't comfortable leaving her alone. A couple of times I heard a thump or a clang and held my breath waiting for a scream, but it never came.

The hair on the back of my neck stood up as I poured a salt circle around myself for protection. I heard the water in the bathroom start to drip slowly, and it told me the ghost had shenanigans on her mind.

"Not now," I said.

The dripping increased at first, and the toilet flushed out of nowhere, but eventually, she backed off. The static in the air receded, and I finished setting up my circle.

I wasn't quite sure what I was doing, but what I did know was that I wanted answers. Basil is mildly hallucinogenic when it's burned, so I wrote "answer" on it and lit the leaf on fire. It was supposed to serve two purposes. The first was that it was a wish, and the second was that I hoped the smoke from the burning leaf would induce a vision.

When nothing happened, I held the burning leaf up closer to my mouth and nose. After a few huge inhales, I felt the floor fall out from underneath me.

When I opened my eyes, I was drifting through some sort of magical cosmic soup. There were lights and sounds everywhere, but it was nearly impossible for me to grab onto any of them.

Finally, I was able to latch onto a sound somewhere off in the distance, drums and chanting. Then, layered on top of that, the sound of a rooster crowing drifted through my mind.

I stopped floating and found my feet on the floor of my stockroom, but the rest of the space around me was still darkness punctuated with pinpricks of starlight.

Then the pinpricks were poking me. It hurt a little, but I was so dissociated from myself that it was bearable. I felt it as more of an idea or a nuisance than as actual pain.

Somewhere from above, a mirror descended. It landed in front of me, and I saw myself as a doll. But I wasn't just any doll. I was a Voodoo doll stuck with dozens of black pins.

I tried frantically to pull them out, but I was no longer a Voodoo doll. Instead, a life-sized doll stood in front of me. The mirror was gone, and I was just face to face with the massive poppet.

"Kinsley!" a voice called from somewhere off in the distance. "Kinsley!"

The voice got closer and began to sound more familiar. Suddenly, I was standing in the middle of the stockroom with Meri at my feet. He was pawing at my foot.

"You're drooling," he said.

I wiped the corner of my mouth with the back of my hand. It was dry. "You're a butt."

"What did you figure out?" he asked, completely ignoring what I said.

"There was a bunch of stuff, but the thing that stuck out to me the most was I saw a Voodoo doll," I said.

"Oh, that's amazing," Meri snarked. "So it's Voodoo."

"That would explain why the protection spells aren't working that well and why we couldn't figure out what was going on," I said.

"So what are you going to do? Because you know she'll probably die if you do nothing," Meri said. "You know, that's probably okay."

"Meri, stop," I said. "What I need you to do is figure out how we can remove a Voodoo curse."

"We can't. You're a witch. Voodoo is different."

"But you can kill demons," I said.

"Voodoo is not our thing," Meri answered.

"What do I do then? I've got to help Reggie," I said.

"I don't know, creature. Maybe try finding someone who can do Voodoo magic?"

"Maybe I can just learn," I said. "I'm sure I could figure something out."

"You'll totally kill her," Meri said. "But I'm cool with that."

I took a deep breath and let out a heavy sigh. "You're right. About the killing her part. Not about it being cool. I just need to find someone who can help.

There really aren't any Voodoo practitioners in Coventry."

"The only active Voodoo practitioner communities in the country are in New Orleans and Savannah," Meri said.

"Maybe I can get one to come here," I mused. "Do you think that's possible?"

"I think anything is possible with enough money," Meri said.

I felt a trickle of sweat run down my back, and I realized it had grown hot in the stockroom. I walked over to the vent and reached my hand up only to find there was no air coming out.

"Air conditioning is busted," I said.

"Don't be dramatic. Maybe it just kicked off," Meri said.

"I'm not being dramatic, Meri. Do you feel how hot it is in here? It should be on. I'm going to have to close the store."

I walked back out to the front of the store and found Reggie standing behind the counter alone and looking forlorn.

"It's so hot in here. People bought a few things and then hurried out," she said. "I'm so sorry, Kinsley."

"You don't need to be sorry, Reggie. This isn't your fault. We'll figure it out," I said. "Let's get the drawer counted down and put up a sign that we're closed for today."

"I'll make the sign," Reggie said. "There's not much to count down in the drawer."

We had to walk back to my house. I'd considered calling a ride, but I figured their car would just break down too.

Reggie tripped twice on the walk back, but I caught her both times. Meri did his best to put a protection spell over us, but even with that, Reggie rolled her ankle a block from the house. I had to use magic to make her lighter so I could practically carry her home.

"The air's going to go out in your house too, isn't it?" Reggie asked as I hoisted her over the threshold.

"I don't think so. You fell in the house this morning, but that's all that's happened here. I don't think the curse can hurt Hangman's House, but it can still hurt you when you're inside it. You have to be careful, but I think the house itself is safe."

"How is that possible?" she asked. "Not that I'm not grateful."

"I don't know for sure. I think all of the protection magic around this place is having some sort of effect." I helped her over to the sofa and Reggie propped her foot up on the coffee table. I slid a pillow under it and pulled off her shoe. "This air conditioning sure feels good. I'm going to get us a couple of Cokes. How's that ankle fee?"

"It's all better. Ha-ha. Thanks," she said as she put her foot back down. "I can help you in the kitchen."

"No, that's okay. Just stay there." I grabbed my laptop off the table and handed it to her. "You get a head start finding us someone to remove the curse. Look for a Voodoo practitioner in New Orleans with a website."

I went into the kitchen and grabbed two Cokes from the fridge as well as a bag of chips and a package of cookies. It felt like the kind of day to drown our sorrows in junk food, so that's what we were going to do.

"You got any corn dogs?" Reggie called from the living room as if she could read my mind. "I thought I saw some in the freezer."

"I do," I called back. "Give me just a minute to nuke a few. How many do you want?"

"How many are in the box?" Reggie asked.

"Twelve," I said.

"Make them all."

"You want ketchup or mustard with them?"

"Both."

"Okay. I'll be there in a few."

It took a few minutes for me to microwave the entire box of corn dogs. I thought about using magic, but that would have been a completely frivolous use. I decided not to do it.

While I was fixing the food, I thought I heard Reggie talking, but I assumed she was chatting with Meri about something. When the corn dogs were ready, I took it all into the living room in two trips.

Reggie was typing away furiously on the laptop, and she didn't stop even when I put everything down on the coffee table. "What's up?" I asked when thirty seconds later she still hadn't looked up.

"I called this place called Reverend Zombie's House of Voodoo in New Orleans. It took some convincing, but they gave me an email address of someone who might help," Reggie said. "I'm sending the woman an email now."

"What woman?" I asked. "What are you saying?"

"Her name is Liberty Bloodstone. She's a Voodoo priestess or a queen. I'm not entirely sure there, but the girl at the shop said she might help me," Reggie said.

"Did she give you a phone number?" I asked hopefully. Waiting for a reply to an email seemed untenable. Liberty Bloodstone could've been one of those people who only checked their email once a day, or worse yet, she could've been like me and only checked it almost never.

"No, just this email," Reggie said. "Hopefully, it's not some sort of fan email account that's checked by her assistant. I'll probably get filtered out."

"Fan email account?" I asked. "You think she's some sort of celebrity?"

"Dude, I don't know," Reggie said. "She might be like that one psychic chick with the big hair and the big nails who travels around doing readings in convention centers."

"That chick's not even really psychic," I said. "They take your payment information, look you up before you get there, and she only goes to the seats where someone with an interesting story is sitting. It's pretty obvious."

"I hope Liberty Bloodstone is the real deal," Reggie said.

"Oh, I do too. Let's just eat our corn dogs, and we'll wait. I'm sure she'll get back to us soon."

"Good plan," Reggie said and picked up a corn dog in each hand. "One for each hand!"

I laughed and grabbed one myself, but I reserved my other hand for chips or my Coke. "I'll leave that to you."

For some reason, I thought we'd have leftover corn dogs, but we finished them all. It was a bit shocking as Reggie wasn't a witch. I'd only ever seen witches eat like that.

She didn't have the figure of someone who put away six corn dogs, half a bag of potato chips, and two Cokes in a sitting. All I could think was that she was one of those people blessed with a lightning fast metabolism.

"What?" she asked as she went back into the bag of chips to polish off the crumbs.

"Nothing. I've just never seen someone as slim as you, who isn't a witch, put away that much food. You always do, though, and you never seem to gain an ounce."

"It's just blessed genetics. I'm not very smart, though, so the universe has maintained the balance."

"You shouldn't say that about yourself, Reggie. You're not stupid."

"Before you hired me, I was working at the diner. I've been a waitress for years. My entire house is a little bigger than your living room. I haven't exactly been the most successful person."

"I inherited this house, Reggie. It's not like I went out and earned the money. I've had a lot of advantages, not to mention the witch thing."

"I had a scholarship to college," she said and blushed.

"What? Well, then you must be smart."

"I guess I was kind of book smart back then, but I make bad decisions. Like getting arrested and losing my scholarship."

"You got arrested?" I asked.

"I did, but it's not what you think. My mom's boyfriend had drugs in her house, and they were yelling out on the front lawn again. The cops came and they were going to arrest her because the house was just in her name. Her sleaze boyfriend wouldn't claim the drugs, so she was going to jail. I said it was mine."

"And she let you do that?" I couldn't believe it.

Reggie shrugged. "I don't think she had much choice. Like I said, the lease was in her name. If she went to jail and lost her job, we'd be completely broke and miss rent. Then we'd be homeless too. I had to do it, and she had to let me."

"But Gunner arrested you. I can't believe he did that."

"He didn't want to. In fact, when he found out later what happened, he went to bat for me. He got the judge to dismiss the charges, and he tried to help save my scholarship. It didn't matter, though. Being arrested was enough to disqualify me."

Before I could say anything more about it, my phone rang. It was an area code I didn't recognize. "Did you give Liberty your number or mine?" I asked Reggie.

"I gave her yours. I don't have any money to pay her," she said and blushed again.

"Right. I totally didn't think about the fact that she'd probably want money for her services."

"I'm so sorry," Reggie said.

"Don't worry about that. Not one bit. Okay, I'm going to answer," I said and swiped the phone's screen to pick up. "Hello, this is Kinsley."

"Oh, I'm sorry. I was looking for someone named Reggie," a woman said in a thick Louisiana accent.

"You've got the right number. I'm her friend. She gave you my number."

"Because you've got the money," she said with a chuckle.

"How did you know?" I asked.

"I've got the sight," she responded.

"So, this is Liberty Bloodstone?"

"The one and only. Your friend's email said that she'd been cursed. How do you know it's Voodoo?"

"I'm a witch," I said.

"Don't mean you know a thing about Voodoo," Liberty said in an even thicker accent.

"I did a ritual, and there was a vision. Plus, she's surrounded by this black aura. I'm pretty sure it's Voodoo," I said.

"I believe you," she said. "So, you want me to remove the curse, then?"

"I do," I said.

"I can only do that in person. It's not something I can do over the phone," she said.

"That makes sense. When are you available? It would take us about twelve hours to drive down there if we drive straight through, and if I can get a car to work…" I trailed off remembering that my car was sitting on the side of the road.

"You know what, why don't I come to you," she said. "I could use a change of scenery."

"Would you drive?" I asked.

"I fly, Kinsley Skeenbauer. First class."

"Right," I said. "I take it I'm buying your ticket?"

"You're a sharp one, Kinsley Skeenbauer."

"And there's your fee on top of that."

"Indeed."

After that, we discussed her fee and then got off the phone so I could book her plane ticket. She said she was ready to go, so I went online and found a ticket for a flight leaving in a couple of hours. The good news was that since it was a last-minute booking, I managed to get a huge discount.

I called her back and told her I'd emailed her all of the information. "I'll see you folks in a few hours," Liberty said. "Sorry I don't have time to chat, but I've got to pack."

She hung up after that, and I turned back to Reggie. "She'll be here in a few hours."

"We'll have to go to the airport to get her," Reggie said.

The closest airport to Coventry was about a half-hour drive away, but that didn't matter. We weren't driving anywhere.

"We can't drive. I mean, I can go and leave you here, or I can schedule a car to pick her up."

"You think she'd mind a self-driving Uber?" Reggie asked. "Otherwise, you can go. I'll be all right."

I could tell by the tone of her voice that she didn't think she'd be all right. "I'll send the Uber."

"If she doesn't like it, she can pay for something else," I said.

"We don't want her to leave. We need her."

"I'll put in for a luxury car," I said. "She won't be able to do any better on her own. Okay?"

"Thank you," Reggie said. "I'll find a way to pay you back someday."

"I told you, you don't need to worry about that. It's not even my money. I'll get it from the house," I said.

"Still, you could be using that money on something you want."

"This is what I want," I replied. "Using this house's magic to help people is what I want. The fact that it's my best friend makes it even better."

Reggie was about to say something, but she was interrupted when Meri came tearing into the room. He ran in front of us and then went behind the front window curtain. I heard him jump up into the window where he remained for a few seconds before jumping back down.

He ran over to us and leapt onto the coffee table. "Fire!"

Chapter Two

"What?" I said and jumped off the couch.

"Across the street. There's a fire. Look out the window!"

I hurried across the living room with Reggie and Meri on my heels. When I threw back the curtain, I heard Reggie let out a gasp.

Smoke billowed from the cemetery across the street. I could see flames leaping up over the tops of the trees. The fire must have been in the center of the cemetery because the tree line along the road wasn't on fire, but who knew how long it would be before the entire area was engulfed in flames.

"I have to put it out," I said and dove for the front door.

"Wait!" Reggie said. "I don't want you to get hurt."

"I'll be fine," I said. "You should stay here."

I didn't wait for her to answer. I ran across my lawn and crossed the street. The heat was rolling out of the cemetery, and the air was thick with smoke.

After taking a few steps in, I thought I'd have to turn back. Just when I was about to turn around, Meri ran out in front of me. He couldn't die, but I was worried that he'd suffer terribly from the fire until I realized he was clearing the smoke and heat out of my path.

I could walk forward without feeling like I was burning alive or choking on smoke. I ran behind him until we got to the fire. Once I was there, it didn't take much to put it out.

The flames died and the smoke cleared, revealing scorched ground and surrounding trees. All of the headstones were covered in soot, but none of them had been destroyed.

"It looks apocalyptic," I said to Meri.

"You could make it grow back," Meri said. "Or you could get that fairy off Lilith's mantle and make her do it."

"Ha-ha. I'm not going to risk letting her out," I said. "I feel that would be a huge mistake. Sometimes things have to burn down to grow anew."

"But what started the fire?" Meri asked.

"We'll have to look into that later. I need to go check on Reggie," I said.

I turned to leave and made my way out of the cemetery. As I crossed the street back to Hangman's House, I saw someone in the yard talking to Reggie.

They looked like they were having a normal conversation, but as I got closer, it became obvious that something more heated was going on. The person's back was to me, and they were wearing a hoodie, but once I was back in my yard, I could tell it was a young woman.

Her hoodie was a deep purple and it brought out what looked like violet flecks in her irises. Some of her hair was peeking out of the hoodie, and it was long, black, and curly.

"Why did you do that?" she demanded before smacking her lips.

The woman thrust her hand toward Reggie, and I saw she was holding a dog collar and leash. Reggie's eyes were wet with tears that threatened to spill over onto her burning red cheeks.

"I didn't, I swear," Reggie stammered. "I was just petting her, and I don't know how her collar came off."

"What's going on?" I said as I interjected myself into their exchange.

"I let this woman pet my dog, and she undid her collar. My little Rosie saw a squirrel and took off. She went around the back of this house. I followed her, but Rosie ran into the woods behind the house. I'll never find her," the woman said. "Why did you do this? Why didn't you help me catch her?"

"I..," Reggie stuttered. "I..."

"This is my house," I said. "Those are my woods back there. I'm sure if we work together, we can find Rosie."

"She's off on the trail of something. She'll run for miles before she stops."

"Well, we have to at least try," I said. "Reggie, you stay here in case Rosie comes back, and I'll help..."

"Suki," the woman said.

"I'll help Suki look for her dog."

"She's the one who let Rosie go. I want to call the sheriff," Suki demanded.

"Reggie here is my best friend. I know there's no way that she did this on purpose. We can find your dog, I know it, but we're wasting valuable time while Rosie gets farther away."

Suki thought about it for a moment. "Fine, but if we don't find her, I'm calling the sheriff."

"Understood," I said. "Follow me."

"What should I do?" Reggie called out as Suki and I walked away.

"Sit on the porch and wait for Rosie. If she comes back, then just catch her and wait. But I doubt she'll come back here. Just keep your eyes open."

I was looking back over my shoulder and saw Reggie nod. All I could do was hope nothing happened to her while we were out looking.

We got to the tree line, and Meri, who'd been behind us, darted out front and shot into the forest. "Hey, was that your cat?" Suki asked.

"Yeah, that's Meri. He's pretty smart. He'll help bring Rosie back."

"So, he's your familiar then?"

It was then that I finally picked up on Suki being a witch. Her magic was very faint, which explains why I hadn't felt it before. I'd been too preoccupied with the exchange between her and Reggie.

"I take it Rosie isn't yours?" I asked.

"Naw, she's just a stray that wandered into my yard one day. I don't have a familiar because I can barely do any magic. My family is from this area, but that's going back generations. I just moved back here a few months ago. I don't have much left in the way of powers or I would have used them to catch Rosie."

"Well, I'll find her. Or Meri will. Don't worry about it."

"I can usually kind of tell when people are witches," Suki said as we walked deeper into the woods. "I didn't pick up anything from your friend. Either she's not a witch, or she's like me and I just can't sense her magic."

"She's not like us," I said. "She's a regular human."

"Are a lot of witches best friends with regular folks?" she asked.

"I don't know. I guess not, but I am."

"Why would she take Rosie's collar off?" Suki suddenly sounded on the verge of tears.

"She didn't. She's cursed. It's a Voodoo curse, and stuff like that's happening around her," I said. "I'm guessing she just didn't think about it when she went to pet your dog. Either that or she didn't know it would happen. Stuff's mostly been happening to her."

"That sucks," Suki said.

"It does, but we have help on the way," I said.

"Help?"

"I've hired a Voodoo priestess to come remove the curse. I would have done it myself, but apparently our type of magic has little effect on Voodoo curses."

Just then, I heard what sounded like a tiny bell off in the distance. "What is that?" I asked no one more than I was asking Suki.

"It sounds like Rosie. Her collar has a little bell on it. Rosie!" Suki cried out and took off running in the direction of the sound.

Oh, no. I'm going to lose them both, I thought. "Wait up," I called out and took off running after Suki.

I didn't have to go very far. About a hundred feet ahead in a clearing, I found Meri, Rosie, and Suki all together. Suki was putting the collar and leash back on Rosie, and Meri was sitting there licking his paw and cleaning his ears.

"You're welcome," he snarked as I entered the clearing.

"Thank you, Meri," I said.

"Yeah, thanks, cat," Suki said. "We never would have caught him without you."

"I know," he said.

Meri got up and started walking back in the direction of the house. Suki shrugged and started to follow him. I brought up the rear as we made our way back.

When we returned, Reggie was sitting on my back patio. She was holding her wrist and sobbing. When I realized she was crying, I took off in a sprint across the yard.

"What happened?" I asked as I fell to my knees in front of her.

"I got a splinter and somehow managed to fall and sprain my wrist," she said.

I healed her wrist as she let out one more deep, shuddering sob. It sounded more like an outpouring of relief than pain.

"Oh, thanks," she said. "I sure will be glad when Liberty gets here and I stop getting hurt. But Rosie didn't come back. I hope I didn't lose that woman's dog forever."

"We found him. Don't worry," I said. "They're on their way back."

Suki emerged from the woods but she stuck to the far edge of the yard. We watched as she skirted around us and headed for the outside edge of the garage.

"Thank you so much for helping me find Rosie. I hope you understand, but for now, I'm going to steer clear."

"Glad I could help," I said and offered her a wave.

"Sorry," Reggie called out.

"It's okay. I understand now, and I hope you get things resolved."

She walked around the outside of the garage and that was that. I helped Reggie get to her feet.

"You ready to go back in?" I asked.

"Yeah, but I think I left my phone on the front porch," she said.

"I'll get it," I said. "You stay here."

"Kinsley, I'm going to hurt myself whether I sit here or go with you. I'd rather stay glued to your hip in case I do something else to hurt myself. I've had enough pain today."

"Okay, let's go," I relented.

We walked around to the front porch, and what I found on the bottom step surprised me. I guessed it shouldn't have, but it did.

Sitting there staring at me was a Voodoo doll. It had black button eyes, an embroidered red mouth, and a huge pin stuck through its head. At the end of the pin was a black skull. I'd read somewhere as a kid that white pins were for blessings and healing and black pins were for harm and hexing. There was no doubt that the pin was intended to do harm.

I picked up the doll, and behind it was a little black jar with a skull and bones on it. Curiosity gripped me, so I opened the jar. Inside was a variety of herbs, a chicken bone, and a dead spider. I dropped the spider and shrieked before I noticed that there was a mirror inside the lid of the jar and one at the bottom.

"What is that?" Reggie's voice quivered with fear.

"Don't let it get to you," I said and quickly put the lid back on the jar. I set the items on the table between the chairs on the porch. "We're going inside."

"Should you leave that stuff out here?" Reggie asked as we went through the front door.

"I'm not taking it in the house," I said. "There's no way I'm taking that stuff inside."

I could feel the icy fingers of evil reaching out for us from that jar, and it sent a chill down my spine. I didn't tell Reggie. There was no reason to terrify her further.

"You sit on the sofa. You should be okay while we're in here. I'll get us snacks and Coke," I said.

"Okay," she said and sat down on the sofa. "I won't move from this spot."

"You know one thing you haven't said boo about is who could have done this to you," I said.

"Yeah, what did you do?" Meri snarked. "Who did you do it to? It must be pretty big stuff."

"I didn't think I knew anybody that practiced Voodoo," Reggie said. "I mean, I didn't know you were a witch either, but I guess you don't have to be born into Voodoo, right?"

"I don't think so," I said. "It's more like rituals and magic that anyone can learn, but I think it involves connecting with things from the other side? Using their power."

"Anyone can learn it?" Reggie said.

I could see the wheels spinning in her head. This was something I was going to have to nip in the bud fast.

"Don't even think about it, Reggie. You're not going to learn Voodoo. You will end up cursing yourself."

"You're no fun," she said and stuck her tongue out at me.

"I may not be any fun, but I do want to help you figure out who did this to you. That way we can prevent it from happening again," I said.

"I guess there are probably a few people who don't like me," she said.

"Is there anybody recent?" I asked. "Anyone who sticks out? Were there any customers who were particularly nasty to you at the shop, or is there someone at the nursing home who doesn't like you? Maybe a nurse?"

Reggie seemed to be thinking about it for a long moment. "Um... Jeremy's ex-girlfriend tried to get him to break up with me," she offered with a shrug.

"There you go. That's something," I said. "Do you think she would have learned Voodoo to put a curse on you?"

"I wouldn't put it past her. She didn't handle it well when they broke up," Reggie said.

"How long ago did they break up? You guys have been seeing each other for a while."

"They broke up about two years ago. Jeremy didn't date anyone else in between because it went so badly. He was afraid of getting involved with someone like her again."

"So, they broke up two years ago, and she's still bothering him?" I wanted to make sure I was understanding the situation.

"Yeah, I mean, she's not coming over to his house every day and calling him dozens of times anymore, but I've seen her drive by a few times."

"Does she live anywhere near him?" I asked.

"Nope. From what Jeremy said, she has no reason to be in the neighborhood."

"That's pretty bold considering he's a deputy," I said.

"I'd say so, but Jeremy said that's one of the reasons she gets away with it. They were together for a few years, and she learned how to skirt the law. She'll do just enough to bother him, but she doesn't go far enough to get arrested."

"That sounds awful, and she totally sounds like someone who might put a curse on you for dating him," I said. "What's her name?"

"Lottie Bevil," Reggie said.

"Oh, I think I've met her. I think she's been into the shop a few times," I said.

"What did she buy?"

"Just herbs and candles, if I'm remembering right," I said.

"You mean she bought the stuff to put a curse on me at your store?" Reggie mused more to herself than to me.

"I mean, my candles and herbs work for a lot of different purposes. People buy them just because they like them," I said and realized I sounded defensive.

"I'm not blaming you," Reggie said as she picked up the tone of my voice. "I just think it's ironic. Maybe. If I'm using the word correctly."

"I don't know why you didn't come to me about this Lottie Bevil bothering you and Jeremy," I said.

"What would you do?" Reggie asked. "Put a hex on her?"

"No, but I would have found a way to stop her. I'm not afraid of her," I said. "Meri would protect me too. I don't know. I just would have done something to help you. If she tries to bother you while Jeremy is gone, I'll deal with it."

"You mean like putting a curse on me?" Reggie asked with one eyebrow cocked up.

"I'll figure something out," I said. "Do you want to watch a movie?"

Aside from almost falling once when she got up to go to the bathroom, the rest of the afternoon was uneventful. We sat quietly and watched a movie or chatted until there was a knock at the front door.

"I hope that's her," Reggie said.

"We're about to find out."

I walked over to the door and stood on my toes to look out the peephole. Her image was sort of distorted by the fish-eye glass, but I saw a young woman with a dark complexion and hair. I wasn't sure what I was expecting, but she was dressed in a green t-shirt and jeans. She reminded me of a college student with her black duffel bag flung over her shoulder.

"Liberty?" I asked as I opened the door.

"Kinsley?" she responded in kind.

"That's me," I said. "Please come in."

She didn't move forward. "There's a cemetery across the street from here. Looks like there's been a fire recently. I'd like to work there, if you don't mind."

"It's haunted, and there are mostly witches buried there. Some of them were murdered," I said.

"That works for me," she said, and when she saw my shocked expression, Liberty explained further. "Graveyard dirt from witches and murder victims will actually help protect me while I do my work. It's true that it can be used for dark workings, but it is also a powerful protector."

"I see," I said. "Can you look at the items over there on my little table before you go? I found them on my front steps earlier. Also, shouldn't we come with you?"

"I just need a lock of her hair and perhaps an item of her clothing. Something she's worn recently is best. You can come with me if you think it will help keep me from being disturbed," Liberty said.

"But what about Reggie?" I asked.

"I think it would be better for her to stay put," Liberty said. "The spirits might attack her when I try to banish them."

"It's spirits doing this?" I mused. "Then I wonder why I can't dispel them."

"They are tied her by something else," she said. "Shall we begin?"

"Yes. We should. Meri, you stay here and protect Reggie."

"But..."

"Please," I said. "Please just watch out for her."

"I'm not sure about sending you across the street to perform rituals with someone whose magic you can't counter," he huffed.

"Then, what would you do anyway?" I asked.

"Don't worry, little cat. I won't hurt your mistress. She's paying me, after all," Liberty said.

"Yeah, see, I'm paying her. If anything happens to me, she doesn't get her fee. I will be fine," I said.

Meri ran over and jumped up onto the sofa next to Reggie. He didn't say anything else, but the look he shot me could have killed.

"Should we take these with us?" I asked Liberty as I reached for the jar and Voodoo doll.

"Don't touch those," she said. "I assume you already did, but don't touch them again."

Liberty opened her black duffel bag and pulled out a smaller black drawstring pouch. She gingerly picked up the Voodoo doll and curse jar before slipping them inside the large pouch. Once she'd tied off the top, she tied the leftover string around one of her belt loops.

"They won't harm you then," I observed.

"I have protection," she said with a smile. "Shall we?"

I led the way over to the cemetery, and we walked between the trees that were undamaged on the side facing the road and burned on the interior side. It was almost like walking through a portal to another world.

The air in the cemetery smelled like ash and burnt wood. It would have been unbearable if not for a decent breeze blowing in from the north bringing fresh air to fill our lungs.

"You stay back and focus your energy on what I'm doing, okay?" Liberty said.

"That will help you?" I asked.

"I can draw from your energy. It will be far easier if you let me."

I wasn't sure I liked that implication. She could draw energy from me even if I didn't let her, but I would allow it. I told myself that just because she could siphon energy from me, it didn't mean she would.

That made me think of Azriel, but I pushed those thoughts away immediately when Liberty spoke again. "I said focus on what I'm doing. Wherever you just went in your mind, you need to stay out of it until we're done."

"I…"

"You don't need to tell me nothing about what you were thinking. Just focus on what I'm doing," she commanded.

I nodded my head in agreement and studied her as she made her preparations. It looked to me as though she was casting some sort of circle.

From her bag she pulled out a St. Michael candle and anointed it with oil. "Fiery wall of protection," she explained. "And this is for us. Also fiery wall of protection, but in a convenient spray form."

Liberty pulled a small spray bottle from her bag. There was a paper label with some sort of leaf pattern surrounding three men holding up branches. She sprayed some on herself and came over to spray me. It smelled good. I detected something spicy and possibly cinnamon too.

"I have a bottle of ritual bath for her to use as well," Liberty said. "I'll give it to you guys before I leave."

I watched as she began her ritual. At first, I spent the time trying to figure out what she was doing, but Liberty kept throwing looks my way like she knew what I was attempting and she didn't approve. I could almost hear her words in my head. *Focus your intentions on my ritual.*

Instead of dissecting her actions, I opened myself up to the magic. It was more than a bit terrifying at first because I had no protection. At least that's what I thought, but as the spirits began to gather around Liberty, the ghosts of the witches buried in the cemetery surfaced as well.

The ghosts Liberty called came to her as if she commanded them, but the spirits of the witches surrounded me. That didn't seem to concern Liberty as she began to sing and dance. The specters that were under her control began to sway in time with her. They were completely enthralled, and soon they danced too as if she pulled their strings with the movements of her fingertips.

Liberty's voice grew louder until the spirits began to sing with her too. Their shouts were deafening, but no one came.

The birds took flight from the tops of the trees, but her fiery wall of protection kept the cacophony inside the confines of the burnt trees surrounding us. We were in our own little world, and it was a world filled with spirits who were ready to do Liberty's bidding.

It occurred to me as I watched them that it was a good thing I hadn't paid her yet. The ghosts under her thrall weren't... nice. They weren't happy or helpful spirits. She'd assembled a pack of angry and malicious phantoms. She had them barely contained with her chanting and strange dance, but even still, she could unleash them on me at any time. Could the ancient witches surrounding me shield me from their malevolence? If anyone could, it would be them, but then there would be an all-out war.

I really just hoped that Liberty stuck to her word and used her spirits to remove the curse on Reggie, and she did. Eventually the whole thing rose to a crescendo. Liberty pulled a tiny ceramic chicken out of her bag, and it became what looked like a hologram of a real chicken in her hand. It was see-through, but it clucked like a real chicken. She slit its throat, and I winced. But nothing more happened than it turning back into the tiny ceramic trinket.

She smiled at me, and the forest around us went silent. So silent it was as if all of the sound had been sucked out of the world. It felt pressurized as if my ears were going to pop, and then the tension released.

I could hear the birds singing again, and the specters of the witches around me retreated to the trees. But they did not go away entirely. None of them trusted Liberty. I could feel it. I wasn't sure I trusted her either.

"We need to take that soap to your friend. She needs to do the ritual bath before she's reinfected," Liberty said and handed me the bottle.

"Okay," I said. "Come back over to the house. I'll get your money."

"Sounds like a good plan to me," Liberty responded.

"You could come in for a drink or I could fix some food," I offered.

"Your house looks old," she said. "Looks historic, I mean. Not like decrepit or anything like that."

"It is," I said and began leading us back across the street. "It's called Hangman's House, actually."

"People were hung there?"

"The lore gets a little jumbled depending on who you talk to," I said as I crossed the street. "But, from what I remember, there was a judge or mayor of Old Coventry who lived there. He was probably both. There were witch trials a long time ago here. Before the Salem trials even. The man who lived in the house hung the witches from the tree in the front yard."

"And you live there?" I could hear the hint of admiration in Liberty's voice.

"At some point, my family acquired the house. Our living there for all these generations was our way of taking back the power from the men who would do us harm," I said.

"Someone else died in that tree," Liberty said. She'd stopped a few feet away from it and was looking up into the branches.

I stopped too and looked to see if I could see what she was seeing. I couldn't, but I still knew what she was talking about. "My mother had ghost hunters staying here when she was much younger. One of them was murdered and strung up in that tree."

"Do you mind if I take a little of the dirt from around its base?" she asked.

"No, go ahead," I said.

"I'll get some for you too. You can use it for dark workings, but you can also use it for protection spells. I'm sure our magics could work together," she said with a smile.

"It's right outside of my house," I said. "I can get it."

"Oh, no, Kinsley. There's a way to do it. Let me do it for you, please."

"Sure," I said. "I'll go inside and get your money. Would you like a drink? I have water or Coke."

"I'll take a Coke for the road if you don't mind."

"Sure thing."

I went inside and grabbed the envelope of money and a bottle of Coke for Liberty. Reggie was sitting on the sofa watching a movie on my laptop. I handed her the plastic bottle of Purification Bath & Body Wash.

"Liberty says you need to take a bath with this stuff. She says the curse is lifted, but you could be reinfected if you don't. You can use the guest bath or my bathroom if you want."

"Okay," Reggie said. "I think I'll use your bathroom. You've got that amazing rainfall shower."

"There are extra floofies in the bathroom closet," I said.

"Floofies?" Reggie asked.

"You know… those mesh puff things you use instead of a sponge. I don't know what they are called so I call them floofies."

"Got it," Reggie said with a chuckle. "I'm going to take my keep-the-curse-away shower."

As she went upstairs, I took Liberty's money and Coke outside. I stayed back while she finished her ritual under the tree and joined her when she turned to me and motioned for me to come over.

"I'm done. Thank you," Liberty said and handed me a small jar of dirt.

In exchange, I handed her the envelope of money. "Are you going to go home now?"

"There's quite a bit more to do here than I expected," she said. "I think I'll stick around for a day. Maybe take that ghost and witch tour and then see what restaurants you have."

"You're going to do all the touristy stuff?" I asked.

"Why not? It must be fun or people wouldn't come here to do it," she said.

"You're right. Hey, if you're still here in the morning, come to my shop. It's called Summoned Goods & Sundries, and I'm right on the square."

"That sounds like a plan, Kinsley Skeenbauer."

Chapter Three

That night when I went to bed, I had a bad feeling. I couldn't put my finger on it, but there was just a sense of foreboding in the air. My bedroom felt cold despite the house being the perfect temperature, but I was sweating at the same time.

At first, I thought maybe I was coming down with something. Rather than using straight-up magic to help myself, I brewed myself a cup of chamomile and echinacea tea. A little nature magic could be just the thing to head off the sniffles. Summer colds were the absolute worst after all.

When I was done sipping my tea, I made my mind up to just lie down. After all, fretting about a slight case of the chills wouldn't do me any good. What I needed was rest.

Surprisingly, I fell asleep quickly. Unfortunately, my slumber was anything but restful.

I knew I was dreaming, and it still felt real when I found myself standing in the middle of the burned-out area of the cemetery. The smell of burnt wood and the feeling of sticky humidity felt real.

At first the din of moans and cries was low and sounded distant, but within seconds it was so loud that it hurt my ears. It felt as though my eardrums would burst.

I covered my ears instinctively and began screaming, "Stop it!" I felt so out of control and childlike. I wished for my mother while I yelled for the noise to cease.

A harsh wind blew me back and stung my skin. I realized my eyes were closed, and when I opened them, the spirits who had surrounded and protected me earlier were there again. But they weren't loving and protective anymore. Instead, rage burned bright red in their eyes. The witches looked like ghoulish versions of themselves, and they appeared to be ready to pounce on me at any moment.

"What do you want?" I screamed.

There was no answer. Instead I woke up on my bedroom floor with my feet tangled in the sheets. Meri was swatting my face with his little paw.

"Wake up," he said. "Kinsley, wake up."

"I'm awake," I said and sat up.

After I freed my feet from the sheets, I stood up and hurried to my closet.

"Where are you going?" Meri asked as I pulled a pair of jeans off the shelf and a t-shirt from a hanger.

"I have to go to the cemetery," I said.

"Now? It's nearly three in the morning," Meri protested.

"I'm not afraid of the witching hour, Meri," I said as I hurried out of my bedroom. "I have to go now. The witch ancestors visited me in my dream."

I rushed down the stairs and stuffed my feet into my shoes. When I stepped outside into the muggy air, the cicadas started to squawk. It was a sound absent from my dream and let me know I was, in fact, in reality.

I looked both ways as I crossed the street even though there was no one out at that hour. None of my neighbors were late-night partiers, and it was too early for even the earliest risers.

The cemetery looked just as I remembered it. A pang of guilt hit me for not using a little bit of magic to clean the tombstones. Surely that wasn't what the spirits had been angry about, but I was about to do it anyway when I noticed something off in the distance.

There was a mound near one of the headstones towards the center of the old portion of the graveyard. I didn't have my purse or my phone on me, so I didn't have anything to use as a flashlight.

A little magic spell that I learned from my mother produced a small orb of light that floated out in front of me like a wisp. I felt Meri run between my feet as he darted toward the shape.

"Meri, wait. You don't know what it is," I called after him.

"I'm not afraid," he said and kept sprinting forward.

I picked up the pace and jogged along behind him, careful to avoid tripping over headstones or tree roots poking out of the ground. As soon as I was withing five feet of the mystery object, I knew who she was.

Liberty's face stared back at me through the dark with eyes that could no longer see. I knelt beside her and felt for a pulse on her neck. I already knew she was dead, but I had to check for myself. If there had been any chance that I could heal her, I would have.

There was no chance. She was ice cold, and despite my best efforts, I couldn't see or sense her spirit anywhere near me.

What was I thinking? Even if I had picked up on her spirit, did I really consider bringing her back? It bothered me that my mind so casually drifted back to using necromancy again.

Satisfied that she was gone and there was nothing I could do, I stood up and retreated out of the cemetery. As I walked back to the road, I made certain that I retraced my steps as closely as possible.

While I didn't know if the crime scene could yield any clues, I didn't want to disturb it.

Once I was back out on the road, I called Thorn directly. "I missed you too," he said sleepily into the phone. "Wait, Kinsley. Are you okay? What's going on?" Thorn must have woken up enough for it to register that I wouldn't be calling him after three in the morning to tell him I missed him.

"I found a body," I said. "Her name is Liberty Bloodstone. I hired her to come here and help me remove a curse from Reggie. Anyway, I found her in the cemetery across from my house."

"What are you doing in the cemetery across from your house in the middle of the night, Kinsley?" he asked.

"I'll explain that to you when you get here," I said. "But, Thorn, there's a body. She's dead."

"Right, sorry. I wasn't quite awake yet. I'm getting dressed now. I'll be right there."

"I'll wait here," I said.

"No, go back to your house, Kinsley. I can find the body. I'll come over when we're done."

"Okay."

I wanted to argue with him, but there wasn't any reason. I couldn't do anything for Thorn or Liberty, and I would have only been in the way.

I went home and sat down on my sofa to wait. I figured that once Thorn and his deputies arrived, I'd wander over and see what was going on, but I must have been more tired than I thought.

The next thing I knew, there was a harsh knock on my front door and light was streaming through the front window from behind the curtains. I'd fallen asleep.

I got up to answer the door, and after wiping the drool off the corner of my mouth, I found Thorn and one of his deputies standing on my front porch.

Lincoln Rains had taken over as Thorn's second-in-command after Jeremy deployed. He was not a witch, did not believe in witches, and found the town's obsession with them amusing at best and annoying at worst. Why he chose to live in a town that was so focused on witches was beyond me. I thought perhaps he couldn't get hired anywhere else, but Thorn told me that was mean.

"I need your statement," Thorn said. "Can we come in?"

"Sure," I said. "Why don't we go to the kitchen. I can make some coffee. I'm sure we're all tired."

I could see Lincoln studying my decor with disdain, but he didn't say anything. It was no secret that Thorn and I were a couple, and he probably didn't want to endanger his recent promotion by making snarky comments to the sheriff's girlfriend.

"Everyone okay with dark roast?" I asked as Thorn and Lincoln took a seat at my kitchen table.

"The darker the better," Lincoln said with a tight smile.

It was as if he was appreciative of the coffee, but he couldn't bring himself to be completely nice about it. I was sure he probably hated my store and the fact that I encouraged what he considered silliness.

"Coming right up," I said.

"It looks like there has been a bad fire in the cemetery recently, but it couldn't have been tied to the murder because there were no burns on the body," Lincoln said. "Interestingly no calls were made to the fire department. I'm assuming since it's right across from your house, you must know something about it."

Thorn looked at me expectantly. It was obvious that if I didn't say something, he was going to jump in and save me.

"I think it was some sort of flash fire," I said. "I saw it and the smoke. I went running over there, and when I got there, it was already out. So, I didn't call anybody."

"A flash fire?" Lincoln was skeptical.

"Yeah. It was on fire and then it just wasn't. I'm sure it happens."

"You still should have called the fire department. What if it wasn't really out?" Lincoln was oozing frustration.

"Sorry," I said with a shrug. "Luckily, it was out, but if it ever happens again, I'll call. I promise."

"That's not really why we're here," Thorn said with a measured sigh. "Lincoln, why don't you go make sure the coroner has everything he needs and then make sure that everything is wrapped up. I'll be out as soon as I'm done taking Kinsley's statement."

"Don't you think that's a conflict of interest?" Lincoln pressed. "Perhaps I should stay and take her statement."

Another sigh from Thorn. "No, it's not a conflict of interest because she's not a suspect. She just happens to be the one who found the body. So, please, do as I've asked."

The look on Lincoln's face told me he knew he better not press any harder. He didn't like me, but not so much that he'd put his position in the department at risk.

"Yes, sir," he said.

"Wait, let me get you some coffee to go. I've got those cups with lids in the pantry," I said.

"No, thank you. I wouldn't want anyone out there to think I was getting special treatment." His statement was loaded, but he hurried out of the house before Thorn could say anything.

"Well, we can have coffee," I said and grabbed two mugs from the cabinet.

"Thank you," Thorn said. "So, tell me, Kinsley, what were you doing over there at three in the morning?"

"I had a dream," I said. "The witches over in the cemetery were angry about something and then I just woke up. It was a feeling. I had to go over there."

"So the dead witches were trying to tell you she was over there?" Thorn asked.

"I guess so. Does that make me a suspect?"

"No. I know you're not a suspect. Finding the body doesn't make you one."

"I don't know if that's the stance you've always taken," I teased.

"I know you now," he said. "So, about that statement."

When we were done with the official stuff, I asked Thorn if he wanted some breakfast.

"I'll take another coffee for the road, but I can't stay to eat. I've still got a lot of paperwork to do regarding the murder, and then a full day of work after that."

"So, it is a murder then?" I asked.

"Stay out of it, Kinsley," he warned. There was an edge to Thorn's voice that caught me off guard. He pinched the bridge of his nose and closed his eyes for a moment. "I'm sorry. I'm just tired, and I'd rather not be dealing with this while Jeremy is gone. I feel like I had to promote Lincoln to his position, but between you and me, I would rather not be working so closely with him."

"I understand," I said. "Why don't you come over after work tonight? I'll make something good for dinner."

"I'm afraid I won't be good company," he said. "I think I'll just go home and crash."

"Oh," I said, not sure of what to make of his rejection.

"Kinsley, don't start," he said.

"What? I'm not starting anything. I'm just not used to you saying you don't want to come over. It caught me off guard, but I understand."

"Do you?" He stood up as he was asking. "Because the look on your face tells me you don't, and I don't have the time or energy to deal with this right now."

"Then maybe you should go," I said. "I'll get your coffee and you should go before this turns into something it's not.'"

"Don't worry about the coffee. I'll grab some at the station."

"You don't have to be like that," I said, finding myself suddenly feeling tired and irritated.

"Like what?" Thorn asked.

"Like you're being right now. You're being snappy and acting like you don't need me when we both know you hate the coffee at the station. Why? Why act like that?"

"I'm tired, Kinsley. I just want to go home and sleep right now, but I'm going to have to work overtime today. I want to go home and just sleep after work, but you're making me feel guilty for not being able to spend time with you tonight," he huffed.

"That's not why I invited you over for dinner. It wasn't for me. I wanted to make sure you had a decent meal in you that you didn't have to cook for yourself. It's not like I'm demanding that you take me on a date or something," I said.

"I have to go. I don't have time to fight with you."

I just let him leave. There was no point in us standing there sniping at each other.

It was still a few hours before I had to leave for work, but I didn't think I'd be able to go back to sleep. I put a breakfast sandwich in the microwave and ate it while I watched them clear out across the street.

When everyone was gone, I showered and dressed before walking back over to the cemetery.

I walked around cleaning the gravestones until I came upon the one next to where I'd found Liberty's body. I looked up and a few hundred feet off in the distance, something caught the sun's reflection and shone in my eyes for a split second.

The locket was in the grass and you couldn't see it unless the sun hit it just right. I bent down and picked it up. It was empty, but there was a little dot of glue inside. It had held a picture at one point. I tried looking around in the grass for the picture, but eventually came up empty-handed.

I put the locket in my pocket and went home. When I grabbed my phone so I could head into the shop, I saw that I had a text message. It was from Azriel.

Are you okay?

I set the phone back down and walked into the kitchen. Normally, I would have just ignored it, but I felt like answering him. Something in me was crying out for someone to act like they cared about me, and Azriel's text came at just the right time. Or, maybe it was at the exact wrong time.

"I can't believe Thorn," I said to the empty kitchen as I pulled out a bottle of Coke from the fridge.

"What?" Meri called from the other room.

"Nothing. Talking to myself."

"Ooookay," Meri hollered back.

"He could have at least asked me if I was okay," I said. "I guess me finding a dead body again is just no big deal at this point."

"Still talking to yourself?" Meri came sauntering into the room.

"Yeah," I said.

"You want my input on the matter?" Meri asked.

"It's probably better if I don't," I said.

68

"Good call," he said and sauntered back out of the room.

I took a deep breath and looked at the clock. I still had a little bit before I had to leave for the shop, so I went back into the living room and answered Azriel's text message.

I'm okay. Why wouldn't I be? In my head, the text read almost as accusatory. Would Azriel read it that way? Would he be able to sense it?

I felt something off with you. I don't usually feel you anymore, but something came through. was his response.

Did you do this to me? Did you plant the nightmare in my head? Did you have something to do with Liberty's murder? The texts flew from my fingers, and I was surprised I spelled everything right.

I waited for his response, but instead of another text, my phone began ringing. I debated whether or not to answer it, and it almost went to voicemail before I picked up.

"Kinsley," Azriel said when I picked up, and the sound of him saying my name took my breath away.

I almost hung up right then. It was dangerous how much I suddenly missed him.

"I should hang up," I said. "Even if I beg you to come back here, I don't mean it," I blurted out.

69

"Kinsley."

"Stop saying my name."

"Someone died?" he asked, and Azriel sincerely sounded as if he didn't know.

"You had nothing to do with it?" I answered his question with my own.

"No. Of course I didn't, and I didn't put any nightmares in your head. I would never do that," he said. "So, please tell me what happened."

"I shouldn't be talking to you," I said, but then I told him about the dream and finding Liberty's body across the street.

"If you're in danger..." he began to say.

"I can take care of myself. Besides, my boyfriend is the sheriff." When I said the last part, my voice wavered so much that there was no way Azriel didn't pick up on it.

"What did he do to you?" Azriel's voice sounded like a growl.

"He didn't do anything," I said. "It's not like that."

"Something happened. Kinsley, you can't lie to me." He sounded so protective, and given how vulnerable Thorn had left me feeling, I just wanted to melt into Azriel's words.

"He just blew me off," I said with a sigh. "It's early as you can tell, so this all happened in the middle of the night. He was just tired."

"What do you mean, he blew you off?"

"After he took my statement, I invited him over for dinner tonight. He was talking about how tired he was going to be, and I thought I'd cook him dinner. That way he'd at least get a decent meal, but he said no. I was a little taken aback by it, and he got upset."

"Upset about what?" Azriel asked.

"Because he said I was trying to make him feel guilty," I said and shrugged even though Azriel couldn't see the gesture.

"How were you trying to make him feel guilty, Kinsley? I don't understand how he could have thought that."

"I guess because I was shocked when he turned me down. I mean, it did hurt a little, but I wasn't trying to make him feel guilty. I really was just looking out for him. I didn't want him to feel guilty for not spending time with me," I said and sniffled.

"You don't have to explain yourself to me," Azriel said. "He should be grateful that he has you and that you're trying to take care of him."

"I think that's the thing that bothered me the most," I said. "He didn't even ask me if I was okay. I mean, I had this horrible nightmare and found a dead body across the street from my house. You'd have thought he would have asked if I was okay."

"I asked if you are okay," Azriel said. "You didn't answer me, though. Are you okay, Kinsley?"

"You don't get to ask me that," I said, feeling a hot anger rising from my chest. "You left. You disappeared. Don't pretend like you care about me. I bet you're only calling to get your jollies off on how upset I am." I hung up before he could respond.

It was unfair, but I was mad. I was angry with both of them. Two men who pretended like they loved me, but neither of them were there for me.

With that, I put my phone on silent, shoved it into my purse, and headed out for work.

Chapter Four

The ghost tour was still going and no one was waiting outside of the shop, so I decided I had time to stop into the Brew Station for a coffee and some bacon for Meri before I went into work.

Since the morning rush had already died down, I didn't have to wait in line. But, seconds after I walked in, Reggie came stumbling in after me.

Her hair was a mess, and her clothes were rumpled. While she usually wore a decent amount of makeup, it looked as though she'd barely had time for a swipe of mascara and some lip gloss.

I was instantly afraid that Liberty's death had caused the curse to return. "Are you all right?" I asked as she joined me at the coffee counter.

"Yeah, I was up late," she said. "Don't worry, I'll fix this hair when we get over to the shop."

"You're going to spend enough time in the shop's bathroom to do your hair?"

"Oh, right," she said. "I'm just going to go pull it up into a bun in Viv's bathroom."

"What's up with her?" Viv asked when I turned back to the counter.

"She said she was up late. She's using your bathroom to fix her hair. Nearly forgot that she wouldn't want to use ours."

"She want the usual?" Viv asked.

"I assume so. She didn't say she wanted anything different," I said.

"And yours too?"

"Yep. Hazelnut latte and a side of bacon for Meri."

"Hey, if Reggie was up late doing whatever she was doing, she probably doesn't know you killed someone else," Viv mused.

"I didn't kill her," I said as my eyes went wide with disbelief.

"Sorry," Viv said with a chuckle. "Too soon for jokes?"

"Oh..." I let out a relieved sigh. "Sorry, it was a long night for me. Or an early morning whichever way you choose to look at it. For a moment, I thought you were serious."

"Never," Viv said. "I'm so sorry. I was just teasing. I can see that was in poor taste."

"Not at all," I said. "I appreciate you trying to cheer me up."

Just then, Reggie emerged from the bathroom with her hair tied up in a messy bun. "What did I miss?" she asked.

Viv let out a loud chuckle, and I had to join her. "I'd like to know what you were doing all night that you haven't heard any of the gossip," I said.

"Gossip about what?" Reggie looked genuinely perplexed.

"Your girl here found another dead body," Viv said before turning around and setting to making our drinks.

"Get out," Reggie said. "Who?"

"It was Liberty," I whispered. "Have you really not heard anything? How?"

"Oh, wow. Okay, no. I hadn't heard anything yet, but I was up really late. I just rolled out of bed, grabbed some clean clothes from the basket I haven't folded yet, and here I am," she said.

"What were you doing up so late? Are you all right?"

"I'm fine. Better than fine, actually. But we don't have to talk about that. I'm more worried about you. Are you doing all right?"

Someone else who wasn't Thorn that asked about me...

"I'm okay. I'm handling it all right. Whatever happened with me somehow pinged Azriel. We ended up talking on the phone this morning, but I hung up on him. I'm supposed to have washed my hands of him, so that's what I'm going to do."

"Well, at least you had a distraction," she said with a smile.

"You're not going to harp on me for talking to him?" I asked.

"Why would I?" Reggie asked. "You're a grown woman. If you want to talk to Azriel, I think you should. He seems to help."

I was stunned, but I felt the need to change the subject. "Anyway, what about you? Please tell me what you were up to last night because the suspense is killing me."

"I was talking to Jeremy. He got a laptop, and they let him do a video call with me. I got to see him, and we got to chat for hours because technically he has a couple of days of leave, but he can't really leave," she said.

"Oh, that's great," I said. "Actually it's better than great. How is he?"

"He's doing fine. He misses home and he misses me, but things are pretty quiet there. He'd expected everything to be tense because they were thinking violence might break out at any time, but it's actually been really boring. I guess that's a blessing, though."

"It really is," I said. "Wow. I'm so glad you got to see his face and all that. I'm sure it was nice."

I felt an uncomfortable pang in my stomach.

"You're thinking about Azriel," Reggie said. "I can see it in your eyes. You want to see his face."

"Shh. I'm sure at least some of these people know Thorn," I said. "I don't want stuff like that get to get back to him."

"Why not?" Viv said as she slid the coffees across the counter to us. "Might make him a little more attentive."

"He's..." I trailed off.

"He's not been treating you like the princess you are," Reggie said. "That's my opinion anyway. Viv and I can both see it."

Before I could comment, or think more, on the status of my relationship with Thorn, I could see that the first ghost tour of the day was about to let out. "We need to go open the shop," I said to Reggie.

"Sure thing, boss," Reggie said with a fake salute.

"You ladies have a great day," Viv said. "Call me if you need or want to talk."

Another person who was concerned with how I was doing...

I tried not to think about it too much as I crossed the square, but I couldn't help it. The excuse that Thorn was tired didn't hold water. I was tired, and I had to work all day too. Still, I thought of him. I'd wanted to make him dinner and make his day easier, and he made it out as if I was acting like a petulant child.

My face must have been a mask of anger because Reggie noticed it as I was opening the door to the shop. "You going to be okay?" she asked.

"Yeah. I'm just annoyed about Thorn, and I don't want to be."

"Good," Reggie said. "And you should hang onto that. Don't let him skate by. I think this is the first time you've noticed him blowing you off, but that's just because it's the worst instance so far. I haven't liked the way he talks to you for a while, and I think you've been making excuses for him. I didn't really notice it until Jeremy was gone, and I'm sorry I didn't say something sooner."

I let out a deep breath. "Let's just get the shop open," I said.

There was a steady stream of tourists for a couple of hours. When things began to die down, one of the witches of Coventry came in. She was smiling brightly, and though I recognized her, she wasn't from either of my families.

"Can I help you find anything?" I asked as she walked past the front counter.

"Nope. I've got a list," she said and held up a small scrap of white paper. "Thank you, though."

"I'm going to go in the back and take care of a few invoices," I said to Reggie. "I'll be back up here in about ten minutes. Just holler if you need me."

"Okay, but..," Reggie started to say.

"I'll talk about Thorn later, I promise," I said. "You've given me a lot to process."

I walked back into my office and shut the door. After turning on my computer and bringing up the invoices I needed to check off, I picked up my phone.

I'm sorry I just hung up on you. I texted to Azriel.

I waited about five minutes just staring at my phone, but he never answered.

"Figures," I said and flipped the phone over so the screen was face down. "It just figures."

I took a deep breath and willed myself to calm down. At that point, I was acting like a petulant child. I'd hung up on Azriel, and it's not like he was at my beck and call.

The invoices only took me five minutes, and I headed back up to the front so I could check out our customer. I wanted to be there in case she had any questions, and since she was a witch, I couldn't just leave it to Reggie. She was learning, but she wasn't quite there yet. While she might never be able to actually use magic, Reggie had taken to learning as much as she could. I appreciated that.

I left my phone in the back so I wouldn't be tempted to keep checking it for a response from Azriel.

When Mariana was done picking up items off the shelf, she brought her armful of goods up to the counter. "You had everything I need. I really love this place," she said with a smile. "It's such a good day."

"It's really hot," Reggie said.

"It is," Mariana agreed. "But it's not every day that the trash takes itself out."

"I don't understand," I said.

"Look, I know you meant well when you brought that woman here, but we both know that Voodoo has no place in Coventry. I can't be sad that she's gone."

But Liberty wasn't just gone, she was dead. I wanted to put Mariana in her place. I could, after all. I was the leader of the most powerful coven, but instead, I rang her out.

"Have a good day," I said as I handed her bag over. "Thank you for shopping with us."

"You too," Mariana said.

I watched her leave the store, still contemplating if I should say something about her nasty comment. She'd delivered it in a sweet voice with a smile on her face, but it was still a vile thing to say.

"That was weird," Reggie said after Mariana was gone.

"It was. I didn't think people would be so blatant about their prejudice for other types of magic," I said.

"Do you think it's because anyone can learn Voodoo and witches are born?" she asked. "Like it's an elite thing to be born a witch, but any human, no matter who they are, can learn Voodoo."

"That makes sense intellectually, but it's still a horrible way to be," I said. "But maybe it's because the Voodoo practitioners work with such dark spirits. A lot of witches don't like dark magic of any kind, and I can tell you that Liberty wasn't working with all good spirits. Even when she was removing the curse, she called upon angry and malevolent entities, but they had to do her bidding because she controlled them. When she left, she wanted dirt from under the hanging tree in the front yard too."

"I can see how people might find that disrespectful and witches would see what she does as dangerous," Reggie agreed. "But to just gleefully wish another person dead like that?"

"Yeah, that was over the line," I said. "I should have called her out on her crap. What kind of leader am I?"

"The kind who is tired and dealing with a lot right now. It's okay for you to let people have their beliefs even if they are terrible. It showed restraint on your part," Reggie said. "People can think what they want even if we don't like it, right? It's not like she actually hurt anyone."

"Do you think there is anyone who dislikes Voodoo enough that they might kill over it? I mean, I know you don't know anyone like that, but do you think people could get that upset over it?" I asked.

"People have killed over a lot less. You know how wrapped up people can get in their beliefs."

"That's true," I said. "I really hope that's not what it was. We don't need that kind of hatred in Coventry."

Later on that afternoon, a car pulled up in front of the shop. It struck me right away as being an undercover police car, and I had to wonder what it was doing out there.

A man stepped out of the vehicle and took off a pair of dark aviator sunglasses. He tucked them into the inside pocket of his blazer. I couldn't imagine it was comfortable wearing a sport coat in the heat even if it was a light linen jacket.

He stood in front of my store for a moment reading the sign over the door and then reached out for the door handle. The little bell above the entry rang as he stepped inside.

"I'd be willing to bet it's hotter here than back home," he said in a thick, Southern drawl. "It feels good in here, though. I don't suppose you have anything to drink?"

"We don't sell drinks," I said, but I felt a little sorry for him when I noticed how red-faced and uncomfortable he looked. Why he was still wearing the blazer was beyond me. "I do have Coke and some bottled water in the mini fridge in the back. I'd be more than happy to get you one. Which do you prefer?"

"Oh, man, an icy cold Coke sounds perfect right about now, if you don't mind."

"Not at all," I said. "Take a look around if you like. I'll be right back."

I emerged from the back with a Coke for him and one for me. The man was studying some candles on one of my center shelves.

"Here you go," I said and handed it to him.

"Normally, I wouldn't ask for free drinks, but where I come from, we don't turn down a lady's hospitality."

"You're welcome," I returned. "It's very hot outside."

He looked down at the jacket. "I'm afraid it's a hazard of the job."

"What job is that?"

"I'm sorry, I let the heat go to my head, and we started this out all wrong. I'm Detective Chance Devereaux."

"Detective?"

"Yes," he said.

"Not from here," I responded.

"No, ma'am. I'm from New Orleans, and I'm here to look into the death of one Mrs. Liberty Bloodstone."

"Oh, okay. Well, Detective, I'm Kinsley Skeenbauer."

"I knew that," he said and extended his free hand, "but it is a pleasure to meet you just the same."

I took his hand and shook it. While it was overly warm, because he was, I didn't detect anything out of the ordinary. So, I let it go and smiled.

"You're not just here to peruse my shop, then," I stated plainly.

"I'm not, but it is a very nice shop, Miss Skeenbauer. Nicer than some I've seen where I come from even."

"That's a huge compliment. Thank you."

I actually had no idea if it was a huge compliment or not, but when you didn't know how to deal with a strange man, it seemed best to defer to flattery. He smiled in a way I couldn't read. The expression was neither malicious nor was it very friendly. I wondered if he practiced that to use on criminals.

"I'm told Liberty was in town to visit with you," he said. "Were the two of you friends?"

He wasn't a witch, so I had to figure out what to tell him. The truth wasn't an option, or was it…

"My friend believed she was cursed, so we hired Liberty to help us."

"You believed she was cursed?"

"Yes," I said, but a lot of people believed in magical things without knowing for sure they were real. It wasn't like I was giving away secrets. The idea was for

Detective Devereaux to think I was just some woo-woo-believing hippie with a crystal shop.

"Why did you believe she was cursed?" He seemed skeptical but yet still hopeful at the same time. I would have to tread carefully, because there was something deep inside Devereaux that wanted the truth.

"She had just been having a lot of bad luck. More clumsy than usual and her air conditioning went out a couple of times. In this heat, that can feel like a curse," I said with a forced chuckle.

He studied me for a moment before continuing. "And for that you flew Liberty up here first class on the same day? Your little shop must do well."

"It does," I said proudly. "And yes, I did fly her up here the same day. She said she wanted to get out of town, and I could afford the ticket. Is there some sort of law against that?"

"There is when you are aiding and abetting the flight of a felon," he said flatly.

"What?"

"Liberty was wanted for questioning," he said.

"For what?"

"She stole something valuable," Devereaux responded.

"What did she steal?" I pressed.

"That's not for me to say right now."

"How am I supposed to help you if I don't know what it is you are looking for?" I put my hands on my hips and narrowed my eyes. Something felt off. "Can I see your credentials?"

He let out a sigh. "Sure, ma'am."

Chance Devereaux produced a small black billfold-type thing from his inside jacket pocket. He flipped it open so I could see his badge and information.

"Keep that open," I said and went around the counter.

"For what reason, ma'am?" He was beginning to get agitated, but that only made me believe that I was doing the right thing.

"I'm going to call the New Orleans Police Department and confirm your identity. You could have made that badge or ordered it off the internet. You say you're here investigating a crime, but you won't really tell me what. I'm going to take some precautions."

Chance let out an even bigger sigh. "Fine."

I looked up the number and called into the station. They confirmed his identity, badge number, and gave a physical description. It was him, so I thanked the woman who helped me and hung up.

"Satisfied?" He raised one eyebrow.

Before I could answer, his phone rang. He looked at the screen and I watched his eyes go dark and stress lines appear on his forehead. He picked it up. "Yes, sir."

The detective started to walk out of the shop. I could hear him saying things like "yes, sir" and "no, sir" all the way out. I wondered if his boss knew he'd come all the way to Coventry. Probably not, given the one side of the conversation I overheard.

I halfway expected him to get back in his car and leave, but after he hung up the phone, Chance turned around and came back into the shop. He walked straight back to the counter where I'd been standing and watching him.

"I need to know where Mrs. Bloodstone was planning to stay while she was in town. Where she might have left her things?"

"I don't know about any of that. She showed up at my house right from the airport, and she had a large black duffel bag. That was with her when I found her," I responded.

"What about the vehicle she used to get to your house?"

"It was an Uber I hired to pick her up from the airport," I said.

"Do you know if she stopped anywhere?"

"I don't think so," I said. "As far as I know, she got in the Uber and came straight to my house from the airport."

"Was there anything unusual in the bag?" Chance asked.

"To you or to me?" I asked.

"Just answer the question, please." The *please* part was a little less curt than the rest.

"All I saw were herbs and things like that. Nothing that would bring a detective all the way to Coventry from New Orleans."

"I'll be staying at the Holiday Inn if you think of anything," he said.

"How long are you going to be in town?"

"Maybe just a couple of days," he said. "You have a good day, Kinsley. Thank you again for the Coke."

Chance handed me a business card with his cell phone number on it and then left the store. Reggie hadn't been in the back all that time because she didn't like the storage area of the store, but she had been hanging around toward the back of the sales area tucked behind a shelf. She emerged as soon as the detective was gone.

"Why are you hiding?" I asked her.

"I don't know. I just didn't want to have to talk to him about being cursed or whatever. He seemed like the type who would be smug about it. Especially since he doesn't really believe in it."

"Well, he's gone now," I said.

"He's not really gone. He's staying in town, and I'm sure we'll see him again."

"Yeah, probably," I replied.

"So, what do you think she stole?" Reggie asked.

"I don't know. Who knows if that's even why she's on the run. That might have just been his way of fishing for information."

"I feel really bad for calling Reverend Zombies," Reggie said. "I took their suggestion, and I got us into this."

"You know what, I'm going to call them," I said. "They are the ones that recommended her to you. Maybe they know something about all of this."

"It's worth a shot," Reggie said with a shrug.

"Do you know the name of who you talked to?"

"I'm not sure. Sorry. I think it started with a C maybe?"

"All right. I'll figure it out," I said and looked up the number.

Reggie watched with anticipation as I called. It took a few rings, but a woman finally picked up. She identified the shop as Reverend Zombies and asked how she could help.

"Hello, my friend called there the other day looking for some help with a curse. Are you the woman she spoke with?"

There was silence on the other end of the line for a few seconds. "This is Cordelia, yes," she said hesitantly.

Cordelia. That sounded right, so I went with it. "You recommended we call Liberty Bloodstone for help, but she's dead."

Silence.

"A detective came to my store from New Orleans. He said Liberty was on the run for stealing something, but he wouldn't tell me what. I was hoping you could help me. Do you know anything about this?"

Silence again. I was about to say something else when Cordelia finally spoke. "You should stay out of things that are none of your business," she said and hung up on me.

"What did she say?" Reggie asked.

"She said I should stay out of things that are none of my business, and then she hung up on me."

"She's the one who told me to call Liberty in the first place," Reggie groused.

"I know. It's bizarre."

Chapter Five

The rest of the day was blessedly uneventful. While there were still a lot of questions hanging over our heads, we were too busy with tourists to think too much about any of it.

As soon as work was over, Reggie left for home so she could do a video call with Jeremy again. They were going to chat while she made dinner and pretend to be on a date. I thought it was cute.

I was exhausted, but I didn't have anyone to go home to. Well, I had Meri. He didn't always come into the shop with me so he could spend the day in the attic library, and I wondered if he missed me.

Probably not.

While I was pulling into the driveway after work, I saw Suki Lavender walking Rosie again. They were about a half a block away, and by the time I parked and got out of my car, they'd stopped at the end of my driveway.

"Is it safe to stop and say hello?" Suki asked cheerfully.

"It is," I said with a chuckle.

Suki didn't move, so I walked down to the end of the driveway and joined them. Rosie was panting a little, and when Suki noticed, she pulled a collapsible bowl out of her bag and filled it with water. Rosie drank happily while Suki and I chatted.

"So, she's doing all right after her great adventure?" I asked.

"She sure is. No more escape attempts either, so I haven't had to go traipsing into the woods after her."

"That's good," I said. "So, are you guys just out for your daily walk?"

"We are, but I also wanted to ask you some spell advice," Suki chuckled nervously. "I'm sorry, I didn't realize who you were the other day. I'm really embarrassed."

"It's okay. I don't expect everyone, especially witches from other covens, to just know me on sight. I also don't see myself as a big deal the way a lot of other people do," I said "So, I'm not offended that you didn't ask for my autograph."

Suki laughed. "That's good. Although I wished I'd known I was in the presence of greatness."

That made me laugh. "You're funny, Suki. So, what spell did you want help with?"

"I'm trying to locate my grandmother's engagement ring. I've looked everywhere in my house, but I can't find it. I need to do a locater spell, but I need it to have a big range."

"Is your house that huge?" I wondered where she might possibly live in Coventry.

"No, see, I think the reason I can't find it is that my cousin might have stolen it. I think he sold it, and now I have to figure out where in the world it might be. But, my magic just isn't that strong. I've even tried doing the spell on the ley line, but all that told me was that the ring isn't in the house," she said with defeat.

"Suki, have you ever found an old key?"

"I did when I was little. It's an antique. I keep it in the drawer in my nightstand. I always have. How did you know that?"

"Most witches do," I said. "It's one of the ways you know you're witch, but anyway, what you do is take that key and tie it to the end of your pendulum. I assume you're using a crystal but use the key instead."

"Really?"

"Yeah. That should do the trick," I said. "Let me know if it doesn't, and maybe we can figure something else out."

"Oh, wow. Thank you," Suki said. "I'm going to go home and try that right now."

"You're welcome. You should come into my shop sometime. I have a lot of things that would probably interest you," I said.

"I'll do that."

"And one more piece of advice," I said.

"What's that?"

"The coffee at the Brew Station is amazing. I highly recommend it."

She laughed and thanked me again before heading off down the street with Rosie. I couldn't help but wonder what it was like to be a witch who had a pet that they couldn't talk to about anything.

With that, I remembered that Meri was in the house probably waiting impatiently for dinner, so I headed inside.

I'm not sure why, but I kept waiting for Thorn to call or text telling me he was sorry for being a butt earlier and that he would be over for dinner. That never happened, and Azriel didn't answer my text either.

At first, the stress chased my appetite away, but eventually, my hunger gnawed through any anxiety I was having and left me feeling ravenous.

I'd been watching videos on my laptop of this guy who intentionally let himself be stung by wasps and other venomous insects, but I set the computer down on the coffee table and headed into the kitchen.

I left my phone on the table next to it since I'd already talked to my Mom that afternoon. No one else was going to be calling, so there was no point in keeping it on me. My entire life, people had lived their lives with their phones glued to their hands, and just like with magic, I tried to distance myself from it as much as possible.

In the kitchen, I grabbed the bread, butter, and three slices of cheese. I took my favorite skillet out of the drying rack and put it on the burner. While it heated up, I buttered the bread.

"Whatcha makin'?" Meri asked as he sauntered into the kitchen.

"Grilled cheese," I said. "Maybe some tomato soup to dunk it in."

"Oh," he said with obvious disappointment.

"I can get you some of that salmon you like while I'm waiting for the pan to heat up."

"Yes, please," he said with enthusiasm.

After giving him some salmon, I assembled the grilled cheese in the pan and cooked both sides. The instant creamy tomato soup cups only took a minute in the microwave, so less than ten minutes later, I had my food.

I sat at the kitchen table and ate it while I watched the woods through my back window. Some people might have been scared to stare into the dark woods at night, but I enjoyed it. Even when I saw things that I shouldn't see moving around between the trees, it made me more excited than frightened. The darkness and chaos out there connected with something deep inside of me, the gift Lilith had given me. I was thankful to her for making me not afraid.

After dinner, I went back to the sofa and started watching the videos again. I watched them until I started to get sleepy. At that point, I figured Thorn was asleep and gave up on any hope that he'd make a surprise appearance.

As I was about to head upstairs, there was a knock at the door. Deciding that Thorn was there to surprise me after all, I went to door and almost opened it.

Meri skidded in front of me and gave me the look. "Fine," I said, knowing that he wanted me to check first.

I tried to look out the peephole, but it was blacked out like whoever it was was standing too close. I took a step back from the door.

"I told you so," Meri gloated.

"You didn't actually say anything," I responded. "And neither did I."

I went to the front window hoping that I'd see Azriel's car in the driveway. Blocking the peephole seemed like just the sort of mischief he'd do. It struck me how much I wished it was him, but instead there was a black Cadillac in the driveway I didn't recognize.

The person knocked on the door again. I went back and looked out the peephole a second time. That time, the knocker had backed up and I could see him. There was a sad-looking man who appeared to be in his early forties standing there with a hat in his hands. He had gray hair around his temples and dark skin that was still smooth other than the stubble on his jaw and chin.

"Who is it?" I called through the door.

"My name is Dante Bloodstone, ma'am," he said in a thick Louisiana accent. "I was hoping you could help me. My wife died and I... I just need help."

While intellectually I knew I shouldn't open the door, the sorrow in his voice nearly did me in. There was no way I could just tell him to go away.

"I'm going to open the door," I said.

"No, don't," Meri chided. "If he's a Voodoo king then how am I supposed to protect you?"

"I have that dirt Liberty gave me," I said. "Plus, their magic doesn't have much effect in this house."

"A lot of good that dirt did Liberty," Meri said.

"Still, I can't just leave him out there. I'm going to help him."

"Just don't let him in," Meri said.

"I'm not *that* stupid."

I opened the door, and Dante looked up at me. His eyes were shiny with tears, and I instantly felt like I'd done the right thing. Remembering what I'd just told Meri, though, I stepped out on the porch and closed the door behind me. Meri skittered out after me, and I used a little magic to lock the door as softly as possible. I didn't want Dante to hear the deadbolt engage behind me, but I also didn't want him to be able to push his way into the house.

"I'm sorry about your wife. She was so young," I said.

"She was, and so beautiful too. I can't believe this happened," he said. "Is that where she died? Over there in those trees?"

Dante had pointed across the street to the trees that hid the cemetery. "Yes," I said. "That's where I found her."

"So, you did find her. I'd heard that and I wasn't sure if I should believe it. Doesn't that seem strange to you? That you hired her to come here to take the curse off some friend of yours, and then you found her body too."

"I guess it was strange," I admitted.

I picked up a slight edge to his voice, but I tried to ignore it by explaining it away as grief. Meanwhile, Meri, who'd made his way down the driveway and was inspecting Dante's car, edged back closer to us.

"Is this friend here? I'd like to meet them."

"She's not. She doesn't live here," I said.

"You paid my wife all that money and flew her down here first class for someone that doesn't even live with you? She's not your partner or a family member?"

"I guess you could say she's like family, but she's my best friend. She doesn't live here."

"Can you tell me where she does live?" Dante asked.

"I can't, I'm afraid."

"I want to talk to her."

"You're talking to me," I said and straightened my spine. I wasn't going to be intimidated. "What do you want to know?"

"I want to know why she was really at your house. No fool has ever paid that much for a curse removal. I want to know what happened to her. Did you lure her down here with the promise of a lot of cash and kill her? Why?"

"I'm sorry for your loss, but I'm going to go back into the house. I found Liberty but I had nothing to do with her death," I said.

Meri had been right. *Mental note to start listening to him more,* I thought.

The tears, which may have been fake all along, quickly dried from Dante's eyes. A flash of anger replaced them, and I could swear for a second that he bared his teeth at me.

"Again, I'm sorry," I said. "I want to find out who killed her too."

I turned the knob and unlocked the door. That time I didn't worry about how loud it was when I used magic to throw the deadbolt. Dante took a big step toward me closing the gap between us.

It was at the exact same moment that I opened my front door and slipped inside. I slammed the door shut again and reengaged the lock.

Dante started pounding on the door and screaming for me to let him in. I instinctively went for my phone and called Thorn as Dante moved to the window and began to pound on it. While I waited for Thorn to answer, I kept my eyes on that window. In his rage, I was afraid Dante was hitting it hard enough to break the glass.

"Kinsley, I told you I needed to sleep," Thorn said.

"He's here. Liberty's husband is here. He's outside pounding on my door and screaming," I said just as Dante let out another profanity-laced shriek about me killing his wife. "I think he's going to break the window. I'm going to have to handle him."

I hung up the phone after that. The way he answered ticked me off, and my adrenaline was already pumping. I didn't need Thorn's help. If nothing else, I could use magic to hold Dante until someone from the sheriff's office arrived. At that point, I really didn't care if it was Thorn or one of his deputies.

As I took one step back toward my front door, Dante quieted a little. It was as if he could sense me on the other side. "I called the sheriff," I shouted.

Though he could sense me on the other side of the door, he must not have been able to hear my conversation. When I said I'd called the sheriff, I could hear him go down the porch steps one creak at a time. Seconds later, his car started and I was brave enough to peek out the front window. I watched Dante back out of the driveway before he peeled off down the street.

I kept watch out the window in case he was just trying to trick me and came back. A couple of minutes later, Thorn's cruiser came racing down the street and turned into my driveway.

He jumped out of the car and ran up to the door. I opened it as he was about to knock.

"Where is he?" Thorn asked.

He was in a rumpled t-shirt and jeans. You could still see the slight impression from a crease in his pillowcase across his cheek.

"I yelled out the door that I called you, and he left," I said.

"Okay, I'm going to have my night deputy drive around the area and be on the lookout for him. He'll call me if he finds him."

"Come in," I said and stepped back so Thorn could enter.

"When the line went dead, I thought something happened to you," Thorn said before taking a deep breath.

"I was just ticked off at you for answering that way. As if I just interrupted your sleep for no reason. It didn't even cross your mind, after a murder happened, that I might be calling for a reason."

"I'm sorry," Thorn said and his shoulders slumped. "That was wrong of me."

"We both need to get some sleep," I said. "But I need to wind down first. I'm going to make some hot cocoa with valerian. Would you like some?"

"Just the hot cocoa, please. I think once this adrenaline rush wears off, I'll be good to go on sleeping."

"All right. I'm going to go make it, and then I'll grab you a pillow and blankets. Or you can crash in one of the guest rooms. I think it's best you don't drive again since you're so sleepy."

"I'll stay on the sofa. I want to be here in case he comes back."

"Thank you," I said, not feeling like having the argument about how I could take care of myself.

I went into the kitchen and grabbed the canister of hot chocolate and a container of valerian root from the pantry. A little magic sped up the water boiling on the stove. Normally, I wouldn't have done that, but I wanted to drink the cocoa and hopefully go to bed.

Once the hot chocolate was prepared, mine with valerian and Thorn's without, I took the mugs into the living room. Thorn was standing in the middle of the living room with my phone in his hand. He was shooting daggers at me with his glare. I stopped short and felt trapped by his angry gaze.

"What?" I asked. "Why do you have my phone?"

"You got a text from Azriel. It flashed across the screen of your phone that you left sitting on the coffee table. I couldn't help but see it."

"So, why is my phone in your hand?"

"You're texting him and you guys talked on the phone today? That's what the current text is about. It's about how he's sorry the call ended the way it did and he'll talk with you soon. And then you texting him. Well, I don't need to tell you what you've been texting him."

I walked forward and set the cocoa down on the table. "Give me my phone," I said. "You had no right to go through it like that."

"I can't believe this is still going on between you and him. I thought we left this behind a long time ago.

Kinsley, are you ever going to let him go? Or am I wasting my time with you?"

"You should go," I said.

"Why? Is that what he means by he'll talk to you soon? Is he coming here?"

"No, Thorn. I'm saying you should go because you're being a jerk. It has nothing to do with Azriel. Not one thing. Look at the way you're acting." I could hear my voice rising in timbre, and I took a deep breath. I didn't want to be having this fight.

"I can't leave you here alone with that guy out there," Thorn said.

"You can," I shot back. "I'm fine."

"I won't," Thorn said. "I don't care how mad I am at you right now. I won't leave you unprotected."

"Fine," I said. "I'm going to bed."

"Good night," Thorn said as I stomped up the stairs.

"Good night," I yelled back down the stairs before going into my room and slamming the door.

Chapter Six

When I came downstairs the next morning, Thorn was gone. He'd folded the blankets he'd gotten out of the linen closet and washed his hot cocoa cup. On top of the stack of blankets was a sticky note with a heart drawn on it.

I crumpled it up at first, but then I smoothed it out and tucked it into my purse as Meri came running out of the kitchen. "Breakfast?"

I laughed. "Of course, I'll get you breakfast," I said. "Don't try to pretend like Thorn didn't give you bacon before he left."

"He didn't," Meri said. "He just left this time. But it's okay because you're going to feed me now."

"I am," I said. "And we'll stop at Viv's for coffee and bacon too."

"Does that mean I can have salmon for breakfast?" Meri seemed hopeful and in a decent mood.

"If that's what you want."

"Yes, please."

Salmon sounded good to me too, so I fried myself a fillet in butter and olive oil and seasoned it with some honey mesquite seasoning. I wasn't exactly sure what would go good on the side with that, so I made myself a couple of over-medium eggs too. It was the high-protein breakfast special, and I was so full after I ate it that I made myself a mental note to start having a high-protein breakfast every day. Not that I needed to watch what I ate, but it did give me a mood boost to know I was doing something healthy for myself.

"You're going to come with me to the shop today, right?" I asked Meri as I was putting on a swipe of eyeshadow.

"That's the only way I'll get bacon," he said.

"Yeah, if you don't come along, then I'll get bacon from Viv and eat it all."

"I don't have anything on the agenda today, so I'll come to work with you," he said.

"You have an agenda?"

"Maybe I do and maybe I don't."

"You're a weirdo," I said.

"Whatever," Meri shot back.

I stopped in at the Brew Station on the way to work, and there was a long line. I noticed the ghost tour walking around the square was about twice the size it normally was too.

109

Word had already made it out on social media that a Voodoo priestess had recently died in Coventry. That little tidbit of information had doubled tourism.

Viv didn't have any time to chat, but that was okay because after I got my latte and Meri's bacon, I needed to go get the shop open. It was going to be a big day for us, and I could already see people looking in my store window to get a glimpse of my wares.

I opened the shop as soon as I got across the street. People came in right away, but I got the cash register ready while they were looking around. By the time Reggie got there, I'd already checked out a couple of customers.

"Am I late?" Reggie asked as she joined me behind the counter.

"Not at all. I opened up early because there were already people waiting. Apparently, news about Liberty's death got out on social media, and the town is crawling with even more tourists than usual."

"Did you off her to increase sales?" Reggie asked with one eye narrowed.

"Oh my gawd, no," I said and playfully punched her arm.

"I was just kidding," she responded and rubbed her arm like it really hurt.

"Sorry, I didn't mean to hit you hard," I said.

"You didn't. I'm just messing with you."

We both started laughing just as Detective Devereaux walked into the shop. "Glad to see you two ladies are having such a good time," he chastised.

Reggie threw him a look, but she didn't say anything. I was about to tell him good morning when he interrupted me.

"Looks like Liberty's death has been good for business," he sniped.

"How do you know we're not just having a good day?" Reggie shot back at him.

"Because the woman at the front desk of my hotel told me that tourist traffic picked up considerably once word of Mrs. Bloodstone's death got out," he said and turned to me. "So it seems to me that you benefitted from her death."

"I didn't kill her to get more sales," I said with a sigh.

"I never said you did," Devereaux countered.

"Can I help you with something?" I asked. "Would you like another Coke?"

"No, thank you," he said. "I'm just here to speak to you about the little row you had last night with Dante Bloodstone."

"I guess I shouldn't be surprised that you've already heard about that."

"Word does travel fast around here," Chance said. "But actually, it was the town sheriff that filled me in."

"You're working with Thorn on this?" I asked.

"Yes. I wouldn't be here unless I had his permission and blessing to conduct my investigation. Did you think I was just sneaking around under his nose?"

"No," I said, but I picked up something in his tone. It was as if he was accusing me of doing that very same thing. Had Thorn said something to him about me being involved in the last two murders? Had Detective Devereaux somehow figured that out on his own?

"Can you tell me about last night?" he asked.

"Dante came to my house. He said he needed help, and at first he seemed so sad. I didn't let him in, but I did step out on the porch. He began to act as though I might be responsible for her death because I found her across the street from my house."

"Are you?"

"No," I said and shook my head. "No."

"That couldn't be the end of the story. What else happened?"

"He thought it was weird that I'd paid such a high fee for his wife to fly up here and help me. He wanted to speak to the friend of mine she helped. When I said she wasn't at my house, he demanded to know where she lived. I got uncomfortable and went inside. Dante started pounding on my door and then on my front window while he screamed obscenities. I was worried he was going to break the glass, so I called the sheriff."

"On his personal cell phone. You didn't call dispatch," Devereaux stated as if it meant something.

"Yes. I called his cell phone."

"But when the sheriff arrived, Dante was gone."

"As soon as I shouted through the door that I'd called the sheriff, he left and didn't return," I said. "Do you know if they found him or caught him?"

"We think he's still in the area, but he's laying low. No, Ms. Skeenbauer, no one caught him after your call. There isn't any proof he was even at your house last night."

"Why would I make that up?" I asked. "And there is some proof. Sheriff Wilson heard him screaming through my door while I was on the phone with him."

"Interesting," he said. "Well, if you think of anything else, give me a call. I'll be around."

"I'd probably call our town sheriff, but I'll keep that in mind," I said with a bit more snark than I intended.

Reggie gave me a high five as soon as Detective Devereaux was gone. "What was that for?" I asked.

"You stood up to that jerk," she said. "I'm proud of you."

"You don't like him either?"

"Of course not. He's smarmy, and he's all but accusing you of having something to do with Liberty's death. He sucks."

"I mean, I hate to defend the guy, but you can see why he might think that, right? I hired her to come down here and she turned up dead across the street from my house."

"I maintain that he still sucks," Reggie said.

"I agree."

Another tour ended, and a stream of customers filed into the shop. We were so busy that by the time I was even able to look at the clock, it was midafternoon. I was starving, but fortunately, Reggie had ordered us some food from one of the local sandwich shops.

I let her eat first, but when she was done, I headed back to my office to take a quick break. About halfway through my sandwich, Thorn came into the back of the store.

"Reggie said it was fine if I come back," he said as he took a tentative step into my office.

"It's fine. Come in." I motioned for him to sit in the chair across from my desk.

"I'm sorry that Detective Devereaux came in here to speak with you before I had the chance to talk to you about it," he said.

"It's okay. I can handle him."

"You should tread carefully with him, Kinsley. He's not from around here, and he suspects you a lot more than I do."

"Suspects me a lot more than you do?" I asked. "So, you suspect me at all?"

"That came out wrong. I mean he doesn't know you the way I do, so he still suspects you."

"What about Dante Bloodstone? That man is obviously violent and not completely mentally or emotionally stable," I said.

"That's true, but he just got into town. He wasn't here when Liberty died."

I had to stop myself from rolling my eyes at him. It was like sometimes the men couldn't think things all the way through, and we women had to be long-suffering about it.

"He acts like he just got to town, but why do you believe him? After he left my house last night, your deputies didn't see him again. He could have been here when she died, and nobody knew it," I said and then sat back and watched the lightbulb go off in his head.

"I hadn't…"

"You hadn't thought of it," I cut him off. "It's okay. You were tired. Maybe next time you're having one of your chats with Chance Devereaux, you could mention it to him too. After all, in the majority of these cases, isn't it the spouse?"

"You're right. I assumed he had an alibi, but I hadn't thought it all the way through."

"I suppose that's why you don't get on my case for getting involved in these… cases," I said with a shrug.

He thought about it for a second. "I suppose it is. You're a smart lady, and you do help me so much."

There were a few moments of awkward silence between us before I finally said something.

"I'm sorry you found out I was talking to Azriel that way. It would have been better if I'd told you."

"Would you have told me?" Thorn asked.

"I don't lie to you, Thorn. Yes, I would have told you."

"But you said that you're sorry I found out that way. You're not sorry that you were talking to him at all?" Thorn asked.

"No. Why would I be? I'm not cheating on you, Thorn. I was talking to him. He was asking me how I was doing, and I answered. I was particularly vulnerable because you left my house after I found Liberty's body and not once did you ask me if I was okay."

"I was tired," he protested.

"I was too, and I'd just found a dead body. So, not only did you not ask me if I was okay, but you accused me of trying to guilt you into a date when all I was trying to do was take care of you."

He opened his mouth to speak but closed it again quickly. "You wanted to make sure I had dinner before I went to bed because you knew if I was busy, I wouldn't eat right all day," he finally said.

"Yeah."

"And I accused you of trying to guilt trip me into spending time with you," he said and rubbed his chin.

"Yeah."

He just sat there for a long while, and at some point, I stopped expecting him to apologize. The longer the silence stretched on, the more I knew that I wasn't going to like the next thing he said.

"Kinsley, I've met someone."

"What?" I felt my heart stop in my chest before it began to sputter.

"Nothing has happened between us, but we have become friends. I'm just now starting to realize that she's the reason I'm being distant with you, and it's the same reason I think I'm starting fights with you. But, that's not fair to you. It's not fair for me to do this to you because I haven't figured things out yet."

I thought about it for a moment too and wiped the tears in my eyes with the back of my hand. "I guess I can't blame you because I've done the same thing with Azriel."

"It's not the same," he said and sighed. "It's not the same at all. You've always been good to me, and the only times you were drawn to him were when I was neglecting you or he was manipulating you."

I felt anger rise from my stomach to my chest, and the heat of it dried my tears instantly. "Don't say he was manipulating me. I'm not stupid, and just because that's the way you want it to be doesn't mean that's the way it was."

"So you were cheating on me," he sniped.

"Not any more than you've been cheating on me," I volleyed back.

"She and I haven't done anything."

"Done anything? What does that even mean? You have an entire relationship with a woman I knew nothing about. You're picking fights with me after I find a dead body because… what? Because you want me to do something that makes it okay to end things? You want a trial run with this woman?"

"How can I know what is going on between her and me if I never have the chance to explore it?"

"Get out of my office," I snarled, and Meri came running in.

He jumped up on my desk and hissed at Thorn with his fur raised and his little tail sticking straight up.

"Kinsley…"

"You know why I kept talking to him? Because the last time I saw him at the Midnight Magic Festival, he said he loved my darkness. He loved everything about me, and you... you... you're just looking for perfection. You're looking for easy. That's why you've started this *friendship* with another woman. Things got hard between us and you started trying to find a better deal!" I tried not to shout in case there were customers in the store, but I was so angry for so many reasons.

"I can't..."

"Get.out.of.my.office!"

Meri raised his hackles further, and Thorn backed out through my office door. I followed and watched him quickly make his way out of the shop.

There were a few customers, some were tourists and a couple of witches, and they all looked at me with admiration instead of horror. "Did you see her run that cop out of here like a scalded dog?" one of the tourists whispered to her companion.

The other woman smiled and nodded at her. I wished I'd felt victorious, but instead I felt conflicted.

"You okay?" Reggie asked me.

"Did you hear any of that?"

"Woman, I braved the ghost in the back to listen to the whole thing," she said with a smile.

I should have been mad, but instead I just laughed. At least I didn't have to explain the whole situation to her.

"I shouldn't have been so mad at him. It's not like what he did was any worse than me hanging on to Azriel."

"It's totally worse, Kinsley. Even he knows it. Please do not start beating yourself up over this."

"But now I've lost them both," I said and felt my chest clench so hard it forced the air out of my lungs.

"You haven't," she said and pulled me into a hug. "Even if you had, you wouldn't have lost anything. Not really. It's not really a loss when a man who doesn't value you walks out of your life, honey."

"You're right," I said.

But deep inside, I knew I'd lost something with Azriel. It might have just been the bereft feeling of having Thorn want someone else, but I started to believe that the connection between Azriel and I was real. So, was it real and I had been denying it because of my loyalty to Thorn? Or was it a manipulation and I was searching for any port in the storm?

"I think this calls for a girls' night out," Reggie said.

"Let's get though the rest of the workday first, okay?" I asked, but I did like the idea of going out with

Reggie after work. I hoped that Viv would be free too.

Need a girls' night. Dinner with me and friends after work? I sent the text off to my Mom.

Should I bring Lilith? You know she'd like to see you, Mom sent back right away.

Please do, I responded.

:-) was my mother's response.

I just hoped that for Thorn's sake, Lilith didn't get too far into her cups.

I'm sorry for the way everything ended, was the text I sent to Azriel.

I didn't wait for him to respond, though. My heart couldn't take it at that moment. It would do me in to sit there waiting for a reply and have him not text back. So, I set the phone face down and went back to work.

Chapter Seven

We decided to meet for dinner at the diner because Mom was afraid that Lilith would get too drunk and either turn the forces of chaos on Thorn or turn him into a goat. I agreed, but Lilith showed up with a flask of whiskey anyway.

"What, you didn't expect me to eat my patty melt without having some whiskey? Did you?" Lilith asked.

"I like your family," Reggie said.

"Yeah, me too," Viv, who had dropped her plans of rewatching the third season of *Game of Thrones* to join us.

Game of Thrones was a really old show at that point, but it had garnered a kind of cult following after one of the pay channels had decided to redo the final season. The actors were all like ten years older by the time they did the new final season, but thanks to the magic of computer editing, they made it seamless. The resurgence of the original show put all the spin-offs that had been shelved back on the table, and the franchise was still going strong. The only show franchise that had given them a run for their money in the longevity department was *The Walking Dead* series and its related spin-offs. They were all on their, like, billionth season.

Anyway, people rewatched the original series every year in preparation for the new season of the sequel series. But Viv had heard through the grapevine that I'd had a nasty breakup, and she put her love for Jon Snow on hold to be there for my girls' night.

"I'm going to put a hex on him," Lilith said before taking a sip from her flask.

"Auntie, you don't have to do that," I said. "I'm okay. I'm going to be okay."

"Where is that one I like?" she demanded.

"You mean Azriel?"

"Yes, now there is an interesting fellow. If I were not a shriveled old raisin, I would have stolen him from you in a heartbeat," she said and took another swig.

"I don't doubt that you could steal him from me anyway," I said and winked. "And there's nothing shriveled or raisin-like about you, Lilith. You're as stunning as you ever were."

"Flattery will get you everywhere."

But it was probably true. Lilith was in her eighties but looked to be in her fifties. Her hair had finally gone gray, but her skin was still entirely too smooth for someone of her age. My mother was the same way. She was in her sixties and didn't look a day over forty.

If you didn't know us, you would have thought we were all sisters instead of three different generations.

"It's not flattery. You are perfection," I said and smiled.

"You really are beautiful," Viv said. "I wish I could avoid aging."

"So, it's done," Lilith said and waved her hand over Viv.

"Wait, what?" Viv asked with a nervous chuckle.

"She just granted your wish," I said.

Reggie just looked at Lilith like a puppy who had been kicked. My mother noticed and let out a hearty laugh.

"Oh, here you go," she said and waved a hand over Reggie. "Now you all will look too young for your years."

"Mother and Auntie, you know how I feel about using magic all willy-nilly."

"Oh, hush, Kinsley. Let us have our fun," Lilith said. "I'm sure your friends appreciate it."

"We do," Viv and Reggie said in unison.

"Fine," I said. "I was looking forward to being the pretty one."

"I'm the smart one," Viv said. "I call the smart friend."

"Hey, that would make me the slutty one," Reggie protested. "Not fair."

"You said it, not us," Viv said.

Reggie wadded up her napkin and threw it at Viv. We all erupted in laughter loud enough that everyone in the diner turned to look at us, but when they realized who was at our table, they just smiled and went back to their meals. No one would dare even look at us sideways. It was a great deal of power, but I hoped to never abuse it.

"Anyway," I said as we all calmed down, "I hate to bring up sad things, but I wanted to discuss Liberty's death with you guys."

"You are so much like me sometimes," my mother said, but there was pride in her eyes.

"I don't really know who killed her, but I suspect her husband. As you know, he terrorized me the other night, so I don't think he's very stable."

"He'll pay for that," Lilith said.

"I know," I said and patted her hand. "But there's also this matter of her being on the run after stealing something. That detective is here and he asks a lot of questions, but he won't tell me what it is she stole. I've gotten nowhere with that."

"I could interrogate him," Lilith offered.

"Hmm. Let's put a pin in that for now. I'm not saying no, Auntie, but maybe we should try something else before we go right to torture."

"The younger generations are no fun," she lamented.

"When Liberty arrived at my house, she had a huge black duffel bag with her. It was there in the cemetery the night she died too. Along with this," I said and showed them the locket. "There was no picture in it, but if you look, you can see the little spot of glue. So, at some point, it had a picture in it. I don't know if it's related, but I just wonder what else she had in her bag. I saw her pull out spell tools, but there could have been so much more."

"Ooh. We're breaking into the morgue," Lilith said with glee.

"Okay, yeah. I guess that's how we'll find out what's in the bag. They must have it stored there."

"Either that or it's in the sheriff's evidence lockup," my Mom said.

"We're going to the morgue first," Lilith insisted.

"Do you know how she was killed?" Viv asked.

"I don't," I said. "I didn't notice anything when I found her, and I didn't examine her closely. I left the scene before Thorn arrived."

"Even better," Lilith said. "We'll find out the cause of death at the morgue when we break in."

"Are we all breaking into the morgue?" Reggie asked. "Because I totally want to go."

"I want to go with you guys, but I don't know if I want to go to where the bodies are," Viv said. "Is there a moral support position in this gang?"

My mom laughed. "You and I can keep lookout. We'll stay upstairs and watch for the law. I'll handle any issues that come up, and you can keep me company. Lookout is usually really boring."

"That sounds great," Viv said.

And just like that, all of my friends wanted to break into a morgue and solve a murder mystery. At that point, I wondered if I was a bad influence or a terrible one.

After dinner, everyone went home and changed into black clothes. Well, everyone but Lilith. She was already dressed in black from head to toe. It was a black lace dress with a high frilly collar that also came to the floor, but she insisted on wearing it.

"I'm not putting on leggings," she said, knowing that I'd wear black leggings and a long-sleeve fitted black top. "I'll be fine in what I'm wearing."

"You'd be more comfortable," I said.

"No, I wouldn't."

I relented because she was probably right. She'd come back to Hangman's House with me. I made her tea while we waited for the sun to go down.

"You know, I could probably blot out the sun if you want to get this show on the road," she said as I set her cup of tea down in front of her.

"We should probably just wait an hour," I said. "Let's enjoy some tea, and I'll show you those videos I found of that guy letting venomous wasps sting him."

"Oh, that sounds delightful," she said as she poured whiskey from her flask into her tea.

As soon as it was dark, we all met up again. Lilith's car was the biggest of all of ours. She drove an old hearse, and everyone but me and Lilith had to pile into the back. I drove since Lilith had three teas with whiskey while we waited for the sun to go down, and she rode shotgun. She insisted on actually having a shotgun if she couldn't drive, and when I told her I didn't have a gun, she pulled one out from under the seat.

"Auntie, do not shoot anyone," I said.

She scoffed at me but lowered the gun down below the window. "No promises."

"Auntie," my mother challenged.

"Fine, I won't shoot at anyone unless they shoot first."

"Good enough for me," I said and backed the hearse out of the driveway.

The other advantage of driving a hearse to the morgue was that no one would question its presence in the lot even after closing time. There would be one person working the night shift in the morgue, and funeral homes often did late-night pickups.

We, of course, would have to deal with the morgue attendant, but that wouldn't be an issue. It wasn't good to mess with people's free will, and we wouldn't want to hurt him, but there was no harm that I could see in having him wander off to the breakroom for a cup of coffee.

Mom told me how to get there, and when we arrived at our destination, I backed the hearse up to the loading dock in the rear of the building. There were security cameras inside and out, but Mom took care of those with wave of her hand.

The locks weren't an issue either. We didn't have to break in because we were three of the most powerful witches in existence. We just walked right in like we owned the place.

At the time, Viv looked nervous and Reggie looked like she was having the time of her life. We got on the elevator to go down to the basement, and Reggie was still smiling. I rolled my eyes at her when she saw me, and she stuck her tongue out in return.

It wasn't exactly the place for those shenanigans, but I was glad to have a friend there to lighten the mood. In fact, Reggie and Viv were more than friends to me. I had a huge family, but Mom and Dad never had any more kids. My two best friends had become sisters to me in a way I'd never expected. I hadn't let any friends I made as a kid get that close to me. I stayed away from regular kids because of who I was, and the other witches didn't like me much because I rejected magic. In that moment, I was surrounded by people who accepted me despite it all.

For a brief moment, before the elevator dinged and the doors opened to the basement, I felt whole. The women around me filled the hole in my heart left by men. I wished I could bottle that feeling and carry it close to my heart forever.

But as it was, the elevator did ding and the doors opened. The basement was colder than I'd expected, and it smelled strongly of chemicals and antiseptic. It was really quiet except for the soft sound of someone moving around down the hall. That had to be the morgue attendant we needed to dispatch.

"We just need to figure out where they store things," I mentioned.

"This way," Lilith said.

"Wait, how do you know the layout of the basement in the coroner's office?" I asked.

"Don't mind that, dear," she said with a wicked grin. "Totally not your concern."

I was going to protest, but Mom grabbed my arm. She just shook her head no and offered me her own soft smile. "I'm going to take Viv back upstairs and we'll do lookout from the lobby. As long as you guys are okay?"

"We're fine," I said.

"Oh, here," she said and opened her bag.

I chuckled as she pulled Meri out and handed him to me. I set him down on the floor, and he ran to catch up with Lilith.

"With any luck, we'll be out of here in a few minutes."

"Don't let Lilith kill anybody," Mom said as she and Viv got back on the elevator.

Reggie and Meri had already caught up to Lilith, so I jogged over the polished white floor to get to them. No sooner had I joined them, and the morgue attendant came out into the hallway.

He had earbuds in, so he almost ran right into us before realizing we were there. I was about to cast a spell on him to make him walk around us like we weren't even there, go to the breakroom, and eat a snack, but Lilith waved her hand past his face, and he dropped like a rock.

"Did you kill him?" Reggie gasped.

"No, he's just taking a little nap,," Lilith said.

"I wasn't going to do that," I protested. "I was going to make him go to the breakroom and have a snack while he worked. I could have used my magic to make him not even realize we are here."

"This was easier," Lilith said as she stepped over him.

"We're just going to leave him here?"

"He'll be fine," Meri said and Lilith gave him an approving nod.

"He'll wake up and continue on his way like nothing happened," she added.

"Okay, fine," I said. "It's not like there's anything I can do about it now."

"Don't be glum, dear," Lilith said as she opened the door the man had exited.

Inside that door was a small vestibule with other doors to our left and right. I could sense something lurking through the door to my right, and I was relieved when Lilith grabbed the handle to the left.

"There's something in there," I said and pointed to the other door.

"Someone, dear. There's someone in there. Well, they were someone. Now they are an angry and confused spirit." Even she shivered a little.

"They won't hurt anyone, will they?" I asked.

"No. From what I'm picking up, they are just hanging around here because it's the last place they saw their body. Poor thing is waiting for it to come back, but at least they won't chance hurting any of the employees."

"What's through this door?" Reggie asked as we followed Lilith.

"It's an office," Lilith said. "Sometimes they store things that come in with the bodies in here instead of taking them to the sheriff's station."

"How do you know these things?" I asked. "No, wait. I don't think I want to know. Just, thanks for helping."

"You're welcome," she said and flipped on the light in the office.

"Why wouldn't they take things to the sheriff's station?" Reggie asked as I surveyed the room.

"The evidence locker is very small there," Lilith said. "Things are just as safe here as they are there if they don't need to be locked away. As far as I know, they only use the locker at the station for things like drugs or guns. So, it sits empty most of the time."

The office seemed to serve a dual purpose. There were two desks with computers on one side, but on the other, the wall was lined with three lockers and a series of cubbies.

What I assumed was the duffel bag sat in the bottom part of one of those cubbies. "I think that's it," I said.

Reggie looked where I pointed, and then walked over to the cubby and pulled the bag off the shelf. She set it down on the floor and undid the knot tying the top together.

Lilith and I joined her and peered down as she started pulling candles and clothing out of the bag. Underneath a few jars of graveyard and crossroads dirt, she found a folded piece of paper. She set the candle she'd been holding in the other hand down and unfolded the paper.

"No way," Reggie gasped.

"What? What is it?" I asked.

"It's Lottie Bevil's name and address. Look, there's a time on it too."

"Like she was going to her house?" I mused.

"Or had already been there," Lilith said.

"It figures," Reggie said, but before I could ask her what she meant, we heard someone out in the hallway.

"What's that?" I whispered.

"We'd better check in case it's your mom coming to tell us someone's here," Lilith said.

Reggie handed me the paper, and I shoved it into my purse while she quickly put everything back in what had been Liberty's duffel bag. I threw it back into the cubby and the three of us plus Meri hurried out of the office.

At first, I only saw my Mom and Viv walking down the hall towards us. I was about to ask them what was going on, when I realized Detective Devereaux was right behind them.

"What is the meaning of this?" he asked in that thick Southern drawl. His voice sounded both exasperated and concerned.

Lilith raised her hand, and I reached to push it back down. "Lilith, don't. We can do it my way."

"What are you talking about?" The concern in Chance Devereaux's voice ratcheted up to a ten at that point. "All of you put your hands where I can see them."

"I have to set my kitten down," I said because I had Meri in one hand.

"What? You have to set your kitten down? What is this?" He seemed even more agitated. "Never mind. Put your hands where I can see them. All of you. Now!"

I watched as Devereaux's hand went for the holster concealed inside of his jacket. "All right, do it," I said to Lilith.

She gave me a nod, and then waved her hand in the air again. Devereaux dropped like a sack of potatoes.

"He's going to wonder why he was here," I said to Lilith as we stepped past him to get on the elevator.

"He won't say anything to anyone," Lilith said. "I imagine it would be too embarrassing to explain. Plus, that handsome yet jerky ex of yours won't steer him back in our direction."

"You're right," I said. "Thorn doesn't even know we were here, and I won't be telling him."

Chapter Eight

I needed to find out more about Lottie Bevil. When everyone else went home, Reggie stuck around so she could fill me in on her boyfriend's crazy ex. One disadvantage Lottie had was that while her stalking meant she knew a lot about Jeremy and Reggie, it also meant they knew a great deal about her.

"She works at the real estate office over near the newest development," Reggie said.

"Lottie is a real estate agent?" I asked.

"She is. It's one of the reasons she has the freedom to stalk Jeremy the way she does, and why she hasn't been fired."

"Why is that?" I asked.

"Because she's an independent contractor. They technically can't fire her because she's not an employee, and as long as she doesn't get convicted of anything, she can keep her license to sell houses."

"You would think they would end her contract or not sign another one," I said.

"Yeah, but not many people other than Jeremy, me, and Thorn know about her antics. She's super careful, and she puts forward a really sweet face. I doubt many people would even believe us if we did tell them."

"Isn't that always the way," I said. "So, the working theory is that Lottie hired Liberty to put the curse on you?"

"Yeah, and I'd guess that's why it was so easy for her to remove it. It was her curse. Probably why she practically ran down here to do it. She was double-dipping."

"Do you think Lottie killed her because of that?" I pondered.

"It makes sense. I never thought Lottie was a killer, but I guess it's not that much of a stretch to go from stalker to killer."

"It's not," I said. "And that's why you're staying here tonight. We'll go to her office tomorrow and see if we can figure out where she was when Liberty was murdered."

"You found Liberty in the middle of the night," Reggie said. "I doubt anybody has much of an alibi."

"Well, she wasn't killed right before I found her. She'd been dead for a while," I said. "If we find out that Lottie was showing houses that evening, it might make her less likely to be the killer?"

"Maybe. I guess we have to start the investigation somewhere."

"You want something to eat?" I asked. "I'm a bit hungry."

"Pizza. Do you have any pizza?"

"I probably do have a frozen pizza in there somewhere, but let's get takeout," I said.

"From Rex's place or from Bella Vita?" Reggie asked. "Cause the diner doesn't have pizza. They tried and it didn't work out. Nobody goes to a diner for pizza."

"I'm thinking Bella Vita and a little detour?"

"We're going to drive by Lottie's house, aren't we?" Reggie asked.

"Yep."

"Stalking the stalker. I like it."

"It's not stalking, it's investigating," I said. "I'll call in the order."

"Already done," Reggie said. I hadn't even realized she was messing around on her phone. "I placed an order online. Nobody calls in orders anymore, Kinsley. Not for like fifteen years."

"Right," I said. "How long?"

"Thirty minutes."

"Plenty of time," I said. "Meri, you coming?"

"Do I have to?" he groused. "I want to take a nap."

"It's fine. We're just driving by her house and picking up a pizza. I'm sure I can handle it," I said.

"I'll nap in the car. You guys would totally get yourselves killed."

Reggie put the address in the car's GPS for me. She knew where Lottie lived, but it was easier to let the car navigate. Meri curled up in the back seat and fell asleep before we'd even turned off our street.

It was a quiet night in Coventry. The only activity were the tourists still out and about. The tour companies did ghost and witch tours until after midnight each night. The evening crowds were younger and a bit rowdier than the people who took the tours during the day. Not by much, though. They tended to behave themselves while in our town thanks to the magic my coven used to keep them in line. They younger college kids and couples that took the later tours were boisterous, sure, but they were far from destructive.

They were also the reason I didn't keep the shop open late. The families and older ladies that did the daytime tours were big into buying souvenirs. The nightlife tourists headed out to restaurants and bars after their tours were over. One of the ghost tours even ended at the tavern.

As we drove past the square, there was a crowd of what looked like college kids huddled around the statue in the middle of the square. I chuckled when I saw that the tour guide was in full costume. She wore a long black lace dress, pointy boots, a black wig, and her winged eyeliner reached halfway to her temples. They really laid it on thick for the night tours, but the company charged more for them too, so it was understandable.

Past the square and through the older neighborhoods, we finally crossed into what I thought of as New Coventry. When I was a kid, you would have been in the middle of a farm field at that point, but instead we passed the strip mall, the hotels, and were headed for the new residential developments.

The GPS told me to make a left turn once we passed the new gas station complex, and I turned into Lottie's neighborhood. It was made up of affordable but nice duplexes. It was created for families who couldn't afford the more expensive McMansions in the other developments.

As soon as we turned on Lottie's street, I saw it. He wasn't parked right in front of her house, but a few houses down was Dante Bloodstone's car. I recognized it from the night he had it parked in my driveway.

Sure, it could have been someone else's car. It wasn't that uncommon, but my suspicions were confirmed when we drove by and I saw him in the driver's seat. I pulled over two houses down in the other direction.

"What are you doing?" Reggie asked. "I thought we were just going to drive by."

"That black car a few houses back, that's Dante Bloodstone," I said.

"Liberty's husband? The guy who came to your house and threatened you?"

"Yeah, that's the one," I said. "I've got a bad feeling about him being here."

"Sometimes the trash takes itself out, Kinsley," Reggie said.

"Reggie… We don't know that she's the one that killed Liberty," I said. "He looked like he had violence on his mind."

Reggie opened her mouth and then closed it again. She thought for a good minute before finally speaking. "Fine. You're right. She's a horrible human being and I hate her, but she doesn't actually deserve to die for stalking Jeremy."

"I'm proud of you," I said.

"Don't be," Reggie retorted. "So, what are you going to do? You just going to walk up to him and knock on his window?"

"Yeah, that's what I was thinking," I said and started to get out of the car.

"Kinsley. Shouldn't you call Thorn or Lilith or somebody?"

"You coming?" I asked as I slid the rest of the way out of the driver's seat.

"Why not?" she said and undid her seatbelt.

Meri jumped out of the passenger side while Reggie was getting out and chased me down the street. He didn't say anything, though.

When I got to Dante's car, I knocked on the window and waited. He eventually rolled it down.

"You better just move along, little witch," he said. "Ain't nothin' here for you."

"Who are you calling little witch?" Reggie said from behind me.

"Shh," I said over my shoulder at her. Her reluctance to confront Dante had all but vanished on the walk from my car to his.

"If you know what's good for you, you'll get back in your car and carry on your way," Dante said.

"See, when you say things like that, it lets me know that I shouldn't leave," I said. "Are you in this neighborhood because of Lottie Bevil's house?"

"You're not the cops," Dante said. "Just because your boyfriend is the cops don't mean I have to talk to you."

He started to roll up his window, and on an impulse, I reached out and yanked his car door open. "Why are you here?" I demanded.

"Kinsley!" Reggie whisper-yelled behind me.

I was freaking her out, but I knew I had to confront Dante. I had a feeling he was there to do something to Lottie, and I couldn't let that happen.

"Who do you think you are?" Dante asked as he stepped out of the car. He towered over me. His dark eyes glowered at me while his nostrils flared.

"I don't think you have any idea what you're dealing with," I said. "But that's not the point. I want to know what you're doing here watching Lottie Bevil's house."

"I guess it doesn't really matter," he said with a sigh. "That heifer killed my wife, and I'm here to take care of the problem."

"Why do you think she killed your wife?" I said. He was talking and I wanted to keep him talking. If he knew something I didn't, maybe I could get him to spill it. "I mean, how do you know for sure?"

He sighed again and pinched the bridge of his nose. "If I tell you, you'll go away, right? I can't kill you right here, but that don't mean I won't come for you."

"How do you know it was Lottie?" I demanded again.

"I figured out the password to Liberty's email. This Lottie heifer wasn't happy when she found out that Liberty was in town here and then the curse she paid good money for was removed."

"How would Lottie have even known?" I asked. "Liberty died so soon after she lifted the curse. There's no way Lottie could have known."

"Because my wife told her," Dante said. "She was in a bad way with some stuff back home and needed the money. She told this Lottie chick that she'd been paid to remove the curse and offered to put it back if Lottie paid her even more."

"She was trying to triple-dip," Reggie said softly.

"Yeah, but this Lottie chick didn't want to pay. She sent an email back to my wife filled with all kinds of threats. Crazy crap that only someone with violence in their soul would say. I would know," Dante said. "And then my wife ended up dead. That's all the proof I need."

I couldn't believe what I was about to say. "Lottie is a little unhinged. She's a stalker and says crazy stuff, but that doesn't prove she actually murdered Liberty."

"So we're doing this the hard way," Dante said. "Don't say I didn't warn you, little witch."

"Hey, you need to stop calling her that," Meri piped up. "And don't you ever threaten her again."

"Silence, cat," Dante said, and Meri fell over.

Fudge.

I knew he wasn't dead because he couldn't die, but he was out cold. My familiar was my best protection. I'd really gone and done it.

"Whatever you just did, you'd better undo it," I snarled.

I shocked myself with how menacing I'd sounded. I was kind of scared, but in defense of my familiar, I sounded like I could rip Dante's head off.

"Are you threatening me, witch?" Dante said and closed what little distance there was between us.

"You hurt my cat, and you have to pay," I said through gritted teeth.

In a split second, Dante's hands were around my throat. He was squeezing hard. Hard enough that it shocked me.

I could hear Reggie screaming at him and feel it as she pounced on his back and tried to hit him. She shook him a little, but his hands were too tight and his eyes were locked into mine.

It was enough that he'd nearly squeezed the life out of me before I remembered that I was a witch and I didn't need to overpower him to get his hands from around my throat.

Suddenly, a familiar voice yelled, "Let her go and put your hands on your head!"

I heard a gun cock, and Dante let go of me. He put his hands on his head, and I stumbled backward.

A deputy named Paul Stuckler came jogging down the sidewalk. He had his gun trained on Dante until he got close enough to put him in the handcuffs he had tucked in the waist of his jeans. He was dressed in casual clothes, so I had to guess that he lived on Lottie's street.

Paul had to call Thorn in to officially make the arrest since he was off duty. He sat in his car filling out his report while we waited, so I never had to explain to him why I was there.

I did have to explain it to Thorn. "What were you doing?" he asked me after checking in with Paul.

"Lottie Bevil hired Liberty to put that curse on Reggie," I said. "I think she might have killed her for removing the curse. Plus, Dante told us that he found an email from Lottie to Liberty saying she'd put the curse back on for more money. What if she snapped and killed Liberty?"

"That still doesn't explain what you're doing here," he said and crossed his arms over his chest.

"Reggie and I were supposed to be picking up a pizza at Bella Vita, and we figured… I figured… It was all me… that we should drive by Lottie's house. It was a good thing we did too because we saw Dante out here in his car. I could just tell he was going to hurt her."

Thorn let out an exasperated sigh. "I have no idea what I'm supposed to put in my report." He pinched the bridge of his nose.

"Put the truth," I said with a shrug. "You know the veil over this town will keep anyone from registering what it really says."

"Oh, and it's just that easy." His voice got louder for a moment. "It's always just that easy with you, isn't it?"

"I…" I started to say something, but Thorn was so angry that he cut me off quickly.

"Just stop, Kinsley. Just don't say anything else. Get your pizza and go home," he said and started to walk away. "And stay out of this stuff before you get yourself hurt."

I didn't protest. When I turned around, I found Reggie holding Meri. He wasn't fully awake yet, but he was coming around. "Hey, big guy," I said and ruffled the fur on top of his head.

Meri just scowled at me, so I gave him a kiss. That made him scowl even more, but at least I knew he was feeling okay.

"We don't have to go get the pizza," Reggie said.

"We'll still go get it. I'm starving," I said. "I think we're only a few minutes late."

"Are you sure?" Reggie asked.

"Yeah, I'm sure. Let's go."

I was probably still a little in shock, but I was hungry. As we walked back to my car, a woman, who I presumed was Lottie, came out on her front porch and watched us. She was shooting daggers at us with her eyes. It was the same look Meri had given me when I called him *big guy*. Little did she know that we might have just saved her life.

"We were just about to throw this away," the young man at the pick-up counter said.

"I'm sorry I'm so late. I just got held up," I said. "Thank you so much for waiting so long."

He gave me my receipt, and as I was leaving, I heard someone call my name. I looked over into the dining area and saw Chance Devereaux waving me over.

For a second, I consider pretending like I hadn't seen him, but I'd stopped when he called my name. That and I was standing there looking him right in the eyes.

Resigned, I took a deep breath and walked over in his direction. "I'd ask you to join me," he said as I approached his table, "but it looks like you're already good on dinner."

"I am," I said and started to walk away. "But, thank you."

"Wait," he said before I could even get one foot of distance between us. "If you have just a moment."

"I…" was going to say that I didn't have a moment. That I had a rapidly cooling pizza and that my stomach felt like it was eating itself. Instead I said, "What did you need?"

"Have a seat?" He motioned to the chair across from him.

"I'm okay," I said. "I really do only have a moment."

"Okay," he said and rubbed his jawline. "I'd like to know what you were doing at the morgue."

I froze. We were sure he wouldn't know we were there.

"I don't know what you're talking about," I said.

"I'm sure you do, Kinsley. You see, I didn't just happen upon you while I was out driving past the coroner's office. I followed you there. I'd been following you. So I know you went there. I'm not sure what you were doing there, but I know I followed you there."

"But…"

"You're wondering how that's possible," he cut me off. "You and your family are very powerful, Ms. Skeenbauer, but I'm from New Orleans. We have a few powerful witches of our own."

He pulled an amulet out from under his shirt collar. The pendant was made of black stone, and it was obvious right away that it was some sort of protection amulet.

"It's strong enough that I can still remember following you to the coroner's office, but it's not strong enough to overpower whatever you did to me inside."

153

I thought about it for a moment and decided to go with denial. If he couldn't remember anything from inside the coroner's office, there was no reason to confess. "I'm sure I have no idea what you're talking about."

"Oh, really. So, if I ask your sheriff boyfriend if anything has come up missing from Liberty Bloodstone's things, he won't have anything to tell me?"

"My pizza is getting cold. Have a good evening, Detective Devereaux," I said and got out of there as fast as I could.

Chapter Nine

The next morning, I woke up feeling anxious. Before I woke Reggie up, I made myself some valerian tea. It only took the edge off of my nervousness.

It felt like something was about to happen, but at the same time, it felt as though something was getting closer. I had no idea what it meant, so I tried to find something else to focus on.

I wanted to talk to Lottie. The only way that I could think of to get her to actually meet with me was to pretend to be a client and ask her to show me a house.

While I was making breakfast, I went online to find a house for sale in Coventry. I actually found one of her listings, and there was a form to fill out to book a showing. It let me request a time, so I picked something that was after the shop closed. After sending the form, I finished making the biscuits and gravy I'd been working on and woke Reggie up.

By the time we sat down at the table, I'd already received a confirmation text from Lottie for the appointment. I hadn't given her my real name, and since I didn't have to speak with her on the phone, I never had to worry about Lottie figuring out who I really was. Not until the appointment anyway. I'd wing it from there.

The entire day at work, I kept expecting Devereaux to show up. Thankfully, he never did.

I only had two memorable visits that day. The first was from Suki. She'd finally come into the store.

"Hello, and welcome," I said as she walked through the door with Rosie.

"Is it okay if I bring Rosie in with me? I don't want to leave her outside."

"Sure. Just make sure she doesn't eat anything. Lots of things in here are bad for doggy's tummy," I said.

"Oh, she's a very good girl. You won't even know she's here."

Suki bought a few bundles of herbs and some specialty candles. I told her that if she wanted to, sometime I'd teach her some sigils to make her own spell candles.

A while after she was gone, Thorn came in. "Can I speak to you, please?"

"Sure," I said but didn't move.

"In private."

"Okay, fine. In my office."

We walked back to my office, and I sat down behind my desk. Thorn didn't take a seat. I wasn't sure if he just wanted to tower over me or if he didn't plan on staying long. I was hoping for the latter. Looking at him, wondering if he was seeing more of his mystery woman, hurt more than I expected. It hurt so much that I could actually feel myself getting angry, but I didn't want him to know that he'd wounded me that much. He didn't deserve to know.

Thorn studied me for a moment. He seemed to soften a little, and I wondered if he'd caught a glimpse of the agony on my face before I had a chance to pull myself together.

"Kinsley…" The softness in his voice made my chest tighten.

I was not going to cry in front of him. "What did you come here for, Thorn?" I asked as clinically as possible.

"Devereaux won't get off my back about what you and your friends were doing at the coroner's office. He insists that you were there and that you went inside for something," Thorn said. "I checked, and someone went through Liberty's things. What did you take?" His question was gentle and wasn't as accusing as I would have expected.

I sighed. I might as well tell him the truth. We might have broken up, but it wasn't like he was going to just hand me over to Detective Devereaux. Despite my parents' reservations about Thorn, he was still a close family friend.

"It was just a piece of paper with Lottie Bevil's address and a time on it. Dante knew about Liberty meeting with her because he hacked her email, but I knew because I'd found the paper in her things."

"Did you take anything else?"

"No, that was it," I said.

"Okay. Don't worry about it."

"You're going to cover for me?" I asked cautiously.

"Of course I am," he said and pinched the bridge of his nose. "But please stay out of this, Kinsley. I don't entirely trust him."

"Why not?"

"I can't really talk about that. It's just a feeling," Thorn said. "I really wish I could get him out of here, though. I don't like him sniffing around."

"Thorn, we're not buddies," I said, feeling my anger rising again. "I appreciate you covering for me and all, but I'm not your friend. I'm not here for you to chitchat with about your troubles."

"What?" Thorn looked stricken.

"You know, at one point, I thought you were my future husband. It's insane, but I did. I even had a vision of us laughing while you put together a crib. I was pregnant and you were putting together a crib for our baby. We made it through it all and we were a family in that dream, but you met someone else…"

"Kinsley." He looked almost bereft.

"Get out of my office, Thorn. We're done here," I said as the tears that had threatened before finally spilled over.

"Did you have that vision before or after you had your little connection with Azriel Malum?"

His question sucked all of the air out of my lungs. He looked so hurt and angry, and I suddenly wondered what we were doing to each other.

"I should hate you for asking me that, Thorn, but I understand that I hurt you too. So I won't hate you for it. It was actually after. It was after he was gone, and it was the reason that I ignored the connection between him and I had ever existed. I had it in me to fight for us. Even if things had been messy and imperfect. Even if we didn't have a storybook romance, I was going to fight for us. I thought that counted for something. But you met someone else," I said. "Now get out!" I screeched at him before collapsing onto my office chair in sobs.

He left the office without another word, and the next thing I knew, Reggie was kneeling beside my chair. She was stroking my hair with one hand and holding me with her other arm. I felt tiny feet jump into my lap and then Meri purring against my chest. The sadness that threatened to drown me drained out with my tears.

After a few minutes of crying, I started to feel somewhat better. Meri's little purr motor certainly helped too. As did having my best friend there telling me that I was the most wonderful woman in the world and that Thorn Wilson didn't deserve me.

By the time work was over for the day and it was time for me to go meet Lottie, I was almost okay again. Other than the fact that my hair had turned blue, there was very little reminder left of my breakdown over Thorn.

Fortunately, the electric blue hair and plenty of makeup was enough to throw Lottie off at first. A good contour job could help a woman shapeshift with no magic needed.

We were inside looking at the kitchen when it finally dawned on her who she was looking at. "You had me for a while," she said. "I see a lot of faces every day, and I nearly forgot yours. You changed your hair since last night."

"I'm sorry to trick you, but I didn't figure you'd talk to me any other way," I said.

"Is everything all right with Jeremy? Nothing happened to him, did it?"

"I'm not here to talk to you about Jeremy," I said flatly. "I'm here to talk to you about Liberty Bloodstone."

"I guess I should have expected that."

"You hired her to put a curse on my best friend," I said. "How did you find her?"

"I called a place down in New Orleans called Reverend Zombies. It's a Voodoo shop."

"I know it," I said. "They recommended her to me too. To remove the curse, in my case. Did you fly down there to see her? How did you actually go about putting the curse on Reggie?"

"She came here," Lottie said. "It was worth the expense of the first-class ticket to have her put a curse on the woman that stole the love of my life."

I ignored the last part and pressed on. "So, Liberty had been to Coventry before?"

"Yeah. She was here a couple of weeks ago to do the ritual. I was really disappointed at first because after she was gone, it seemed like she hadn't done anything. But man, when that curse kicked it, it really kicked in. That was until you had to go and pay her to remove it."

"Sorry, Lottie, but you can't curse my best friend over your ex-boyfriend," I said. "But, anyway. You got an email from her offering to put the curse back if you paid her again, and that made you angry. Last night, out in front of your house, Dante told me he found the email. That's why he was there to hurt you."

"And you think I killed her because I sent her an angry email?"

"You threatened to kill her in the email, Lottie."

"I was really upset, but it's ridiculous that you think it was me rather than her obviously violent husband. I'm sure she probably did something to set him off, and he's just here covering his tracks."

"But where were you the night she died?"

"Ugh, this again," Lottie said and rolled her eyes. "Look, I was showing houses to clients until after ten that night. We check into and out of each of these houses, so there's proof I was working."

"What about after ten? I didn't find her body until nearly morning."

"From what I heard, you found her around three in the morning and she'd already been dead for hours. I was at the tavern until almost two because I met a guy. I have receipts that I've already shown to the cops. Plus, I went home with the guy, and my car's GPS tracking confirms it."

I had nothing. I was sure it was her.

"Anything else?" she asked smugly. "I'm sure you're not actually interested in this house, but if you are ever interested in selling that architectural and historical wonder you live in, please give me a call." Lottie handed me a business card as she ushered me toward the door.

"I would never sell Hangman's House, and even if I did, Lottie, you put a curse on my best friend."

"But I'm the best real estate agent in Coventry. No one else could get you a better deal."

And with that, she was in her car driving away while I just stood there on the house's front porch wondering what was next. I was shaken. Finding out that I was wrong about Lottie had upset me again, and I was already on thin ice emotionally because of earlier with Thorn.

I decided to take a walk around the neighborhood to calm my nerves before I got behind the wheel to drive. I also made a mental note to really look into the self-driving feature available for my car. I could finally see its benefit.

All of the houses in that neighborhood looked almost identical. The only real differences were the color and which side the garage was on. Still, it was quiet, and the boring atmosphere helped steady my nerves considerably.

At the end of the neighborhood, there was even a wooded area with a short walking trail. A little ways in, I found myself standing on a small wood footbridge staring down at what was most likely a manmade stream. Still, it was lovely watching the water swirl over and around the perfectly arranged boulders.

It was so lovely, in fact, that I didn't even hear someone walk up behind me.

Chapter Ten

The knife went into my back so swiftly and smoothly that at first I didn't realize I'd been stabbed. Searing pain that radiated down my arm and back was the first real clue that anything was wrong.

I spun around and nearly fell over the railing of the bridge, but I did manage to catch myself in time with the arm that was on the other side of where the knife went into my back.

Dante stood there staring at me with both hate and amusement lighting up his eyes. "You should've learned to stay out of things, little witch," he said before turning and running off.

The pain made its way down to my lower back, and my knees buckled underneath me. I reached for the knife with my good arm and screamed as I pulled it from my back.

The pain was worse than anything I'd ever felt in my life. But that wasn't the worst part. The worst part was that no matter how hard I tried, I couldn't heal the wound. The dagger burned my hand, and I dropped it. It was cursed with some sort of magic I couldn't counter.

I managed to get my phone out and tried to call for help, but my vision was too blurred to dial. I tried to give the phone a voice command to call for my mother, but all I could do was choke.

I called out for her in my mind, but even that was going dark. Black tentacles swam in the corners of my vision as the gloom closed in on me.

Again, I tried to heal myself, but even giving it everything I had, I was only able to pull myself back up to my knees. There must have been some sort of magical poison on the knife that was both sentient and malevolent, because as soon as I got even a hint of strength, it surged again.

I fell over again and wrapped my arms around myself. Meri had wanted to come with me, but I'd told him people didn't bring their kittens to real estate showings. He'd insisted on waiting in the car, but I'd told him no. I didn't want anyone calling the sheriff because there was a kitten in a car when it was so hot out.

I wished I'd brought him with me. He probably couldn't have healed me, but at least I wouldn't be dying alone.

I wished that I had more time left in Coventry and that I'd never left. Hey, I couldn't take back the past, but I was dying. That meant I could wish for whatever I wanted.

The last thing I thought about before I couldn't even hold onto a thought anymore was my wish that I could apologize to Thorn. I wanted to tell him that I was sorry for yelling at him and that we were all human. I understood that then. We all made mistakes, and in the end, it didn't matter enough to hold a grudge. I wanted to tell him that I hoped he would be happy, even if it wasn't with me, for the rest of his days, and maybe we could be friends on the other side. Maybe I would see him again.

I was nearly gone, I could even see a light opening up somewhere off in the distance, when I swore I felt a hand slide under my head.

Cold skin pressed against my neck and shoulder.

A cool cheek against mine.

"You smell like flowers and spun sugar, my love," a voice whispered from a million miles away.

I could barely move my arm, but with great effort, I reached my hand up and felt skin as smooth and cool as porcelain.

Azriel.

As I lay dying, my mind had conjured him to comfort me. I had no strength left in me, but the last of it I used to weep with joy and regret. The two swirled together like ice cream on a hot summer day. It was so sweet, but soon it would melt away.

It hit me that maybe he wasn't my imagination. Perhaps our connection was so strong that he was there. In spirit, anyway. Wherever he was, he was thinking of me too.

"I'm here," his voice murmured from a distance again.

"I know," I tried to say, but nothing would come out. It was no more than a dry scratch of syllables.

"Kinsley, baby, I'm really here. I can help you. I can try anyway." His voice was now frantic with fear, and it made my heart speed up too. "I need you to tell me it's okay." His hand squeezed mine. "Please tell me it's okay to save you. I can't lose you forever."

I could barely nod my head yes, but I tried. I squeezed his hand with what little I had left in me. It was barely anything, but his fear had spiked my adrenaline. One last push before it was all gone.

"Okay," he said softly. "Hold on, baby."

At first, I just felt his cool wrist pressed against my lips. It took me a moment to realize there was something salty and wet too.

Blood.

Just a little, but enough that at first, it made me want to recoil. I didn't have the strength to even flinch away, but I didn't accept it at first either.

Then, I started to hear the sound of his voice in it and feel the beating of his heart. It was a myth that vampires' hearts didn't beat. They did, but it was still mostly a memory.

As his blood began to run through my veins, the darkness started to recede. My body no longer felt like lead, and as his essence entwined with mine, my heart jumped back to life. It had nearly been nothing more than a memory, but then it thundered like the sound of horse hooves on dirt.

Instinctively and subconsciously, I began to chant a healing spell. I said the words over and over as I tried to fight back the poison.

"That's it," Azriel said. He pulled me closer until I was nearly on his lap. "Fight it, Kinsley. You are stronger than this."

Everything was a haze for a while as my body came back to life and Azriel's blood chased the magical poison out of every corner of my being. My whole world was his arms wrapped around me anchoring me to this side.

"How did you do that?" I was finally able to ask. "How could you save me?"

Azriel smiled and pushed a lock of my hair away from my face. I wondered what color it was after all of that, but I would wait to find out.

"My blood is life, and as I'd hoped, it was enough to counteract the death magic poison," he said and kissed the tip of my nose. "And now you're back."

"How did you know what was happening to me?"

"I'm a vampire, Kinsley. I'm no stranger to New Orleans. I've seen a dagger like that before. It's death magic. Even I could see that."

"Thank you," I said and tried to sit up.

Azriel helped me gently. "Take it easy, baby. You're out of the woods, but your strength will take time."

"I'm not out of the woods," I said with a chuckle. "We are still very much in the woods."

Azriel's smile widened. "Well, if you can joke, then you're probably going to live."

"Am I a vampire?" I asked, suddenly realizing the meaning of his cure.

"No," he said with a smile and pulled me even closer. "But, if a vampire ever bit you, I think that might be possible."

"Oh, okay," I said and let my head fall against his chest. "I can hear your heart beating."

"That's your heart, my love."

It took me a moment to realize what he was saying. Not that our hearts were beating in time, because they were doing that too, but that his now belonged to me. "That was really cheesy," I said even as I stroked his cheek.

He caught my hand in his and started to laugh. "Let me help you get to your feet. I think you're strong enough to get home now."

"You might need to give me a ride. I don't think I'm in any condition to drive."

"I'm on my bike," Azriel said. "I can drive your car?"

"Sure. I mean, it can practically drive itself. I guess you could just follow me home. Are you staying?"

"I'll drive your car and come back for my bike later," he said. "And yes, I'm staying. I can accompany you home if you'll have me."

I was quiet most of the drive back to Hangman's House. Not because I didn't want to talk to him, but because I was exhausted. I needed food and rest.

"Where were you? Why didn't you answer my call?" I finally asked as we neared my street.

"I was answering your call, Kinsley dear. Ever since you hung up on me, I've been riding. I didn't answer your calls because I was trying to get to you."

"If you've been riding all this time, you must have been far away," I said.

"I was. We were on the West Coast near the Canadian border," he said. "I got here as fast as I could."

"When you called once, Thorn was at my house. We fought over it," I said.

"I'm sorry for that. I never meant to cause you any pain, but when you didn't answer, I just rode harder."

"It's all right. He and I broke up. He actually met someone else," I said.

"I'm so sorry, Kinsley."

"No, you're not." It was more of a tease than an accusation, but I supposed the tone of my voice didn't accurately convey either.

"Kinsley, no matter how much I want you, I would never do anything to hurt you. If he was what you wanted, even if I can't stand the way he treats you, I wouldn't come between you."

"But you're here," I said.

"Should I go back?" he asked seriously.

"No," I said and then noticed something sitting at the end of my driveway as we got close to my house. "Azriel, pull over."

"Kinsley, what's going on?" But even as he asked, he pulled the car over to the shoulder.

"Look at my driveway. There's something... someone there."

I started to get out of the car. "Honey, wait," Azriel warned.

But I was already halfway out. "I have to see who that is."

I shut my door and started walking toward my house.

"You are so stubborn," Azriel said, but there was no malice in his voice.

I stopped in the middle of the road. As soon as I saw that face, I knew who it was. He had to have laid some sort of trap, but did that make sense? Dante must have thought I was dead for sure, so why was he lying there at the end of my driveway.

"It's him," I barely squeaked out. "It's the man who stabbed me."

Some sort of primal growl escaped from Azriel. "Get back in the car," he snarled.

"No, I'm..."

"Get back in the car, Kinsley. Do it now."

When I looked at Azriel, his eyes had gone completely black. He looked absolutely feral, and I could feel the violence rolling off of him in waves.

Instead of arguing more, I did as he said. I got back in the car and watched.

As soon as my door closed, Azriel shot forward with supernatural speed. He closed in on Dante so fast it was almost as if he'd teleported. I was sure a regular human watching him would have believed he had.

He bent to examine Dante, and then turned and started walking back to the car. Confused, I got out and met him halfway.

"He's dead," Azriel said before I could speak. "Someone slit his throat."

"In my driveway?"

"It looks that way. He bled out there."

That complicated things considerably. I was sure after Dante stabbed me in the back that he was the killer. Lottie had been right about the violence in him. Even a regular human, well, as regular as anyone as crazy as she was could be, could see it in him.

But he was dead. In my driveway. "I'll call the sheriff," I said regretfully.

"You don't have to," Azriel said softly. "I can take care of this. They'll never find him."

"What?" I was shocked, but a small part of me began to consider it.

"After what you've just been through, wouldn't it be easier for everyone if he just went away?"

"It would be…" I said. "But I can't do that. He's not the killer, obviously. That means they're still out there. If hiding Dante's death meant that someone else died, I could never forgive myself."

"You're going to be implicated in this," Azriel warned.

"I know, but it will be fine. I know it will. I have you here with me, I'll be okay."

Azriel nodded, and I pulled out my phone. I called the county dispatch instead of calling Thorn directly.

"His throat is cut and there is more of his blood on my driveway than in him," I said when the dispatcher asked me if I was sure he was dead for the third time.

After I got off the phone with her, Azriel and I went into the house and waited. Meri wasn't in the house, and I began to worry. Fortunately a couple of minutes later, he came bounding down the street from the opposite direction.

He saw Dante's body and gave it a wide berth. I'd been watching out the front window for the sheriff's office cruisers to show up, so I let him in as soon as he was on the porch.

"What the heck!" Meri shouted, but it came out more as a little squeak, when he barreled through the front door. "You were dying. I tried to get to you, but by the time I got there, you were gone."

"Azriel saved me," I said, and it appeared Meri finally noticed Azriel seated on the sofa. "We came right back here. I'm sorry, Meri. I didn't know you were out looking for me."

"Is that they guy who stabbed you in the driveway?" Meri asked. Somehow, he just knew. Cats knew things.

"It is," I said.

"Did vampy here kill him? Because, thanks, dude, but I wish I could have helped."

"Nope, he was dead when we got here," I said.

"So, he tried to kill you, and the, someone killed him. Here," Meri said.

"Yeah," I answered. "That's about the sum of it."

"Do you think they'll arrest you?" Meri asked.

"I won't let that happen," Azriel said.

"I like your spirit," Meri said. "But I'm not sure if it's a good idea to kill the entire Coventry Sheriff's Department."

"It will be okay," I said. "I hope they don't arrest me, though, because I really need some food and to rest."

"Cat, get her to sit down," Azriel said. "I'm going into the kitchen to cook."

"Can you make some bacon while you're in there?" Meri asked hopefully.

"If you get her to sit down, I'll make you bacon, cat."

Meri just glared at me.

"Fine. I'll sit until they get here," I said.

"No, I will handle them too," Azriel said. "Unless they have a warrant for your arrest or to come in here, you're not going out there and they're not coming in here."

"You're awfully bossy," I said.

"That's because I'm used to being the boss," he said.

"Well, don't get used to it around here. I'm only listening to you because I'm tired," I said and plopped down on the sofa.

Azriel was in the middle of making pasta when someone from the sheriff's department knocked on the front door. I was never sure who it was because Azriel sent me into the kitchen before he answered it. He was probably afraid it was Thorn and I'd either be coaxed into going outside or letting him in. As it was, he handled them.

A short while later, there was another knock at the door, and it was a good thing that Azriel made a huge pot of pasta because it was my mom, dad, and Lilith. Amelda came too, but she sat on the porch glaring at the deputies and Thorn. She was daring them to try and come inside, and of course, they steered clear of her.

Azriel took her a huge plate of pasta and a glass of fresh lemonade. Remy tried to get her to come in, but she insisted she was fine keeping watch over what was going on in my driveway.

"You're okay?" Mom asked me for the fifth time.

"I am," I said. "It was death magic in the knife, but Azriel's blood cured it."

"At least is was just a regular death magic poison and not a zombie curse," Dad said before eating another huge forkful of the pasta.

"What?" I asked. "I haven't heard that story, have I?"

"Your mom got turned into a zombie and she had to have vampire blood to save her," Lilith said before holding up her empty wine glass. Azriel actually got up and filled it for her without being asked. "Ooh, I like him already."

"Don't get used to it," I said. "He's not normally so subservient."

"Even better," Lilith said with a wicked smile.

"He is with you," Meri snarked. "He's always getting you stuff and taking care of you. Every time I see him, he's getting you wine or making you snacks."

Meri was right, and I hadn't realized it. Azriel was always trying to take care of me. He was the hard-as-nails leader of a vampire biker gang, and he was always trying to make me food or doing whatever it took to make me okay.

"Huh," I said with a chuckle. "Thank you, Azriel. Thank you so much for everything."

"I really like this shade of red," Mom said as she tugged on a strand of my hair. "It suits you."

"Red again," I said and pulled a strand out to examine it. "Very dark red, but at least it's not blue anymore."

"Blue. What happened?" My father suddenly seemed agitated. "Who…"

"It's okay, Daddy. I'm okay," I said and looked over at Azriel. "Really, guys. I'm going to be all right."

"Is he staying here with you?" Mom asked.

"I don't know," I said with a shrug. "Azriel, are you staying here with me or should I get you a room at the Holiday Inn?"

"Oh, stop," Lilith said with a waggle of her perfectly drawn-on eyebrows. "We all know he's staying here. He saved your life, after all, and only a truly dead person could resist a man that gorgeous. Thank you for the meal, but I'll be dragging your parents and Amelda out of here now. We'll let the sheriff know that you'll make your formal statement tomorrow. Enjoy your evening, kids." The last part she said with a wink.

When everyone was gone for the evening, Meri just said, "gross," and went upstairs.

"You have leaves in your hair," Azriel said with a smile.

I reached up and touched my head. He was right. I was caked with dirt and leaves from rolling around on the ground. "I need a shower," I said.

"Go ahead. I've got all the time in the world. Literally," he said with a smile.

I showered quickly, and after much debate over what to wear, I settled on a fresh t-shirt and clean jeans. I didn't want to look like I was trying too hard for

Azriel. I worried he would find it disingenuous. Plus, I was too tired to get all dressed up to sit in my living room.

"I love you best just like that," Azriel said as I came down the stairs.

He'd started a fire and was just standing there staring into it before I came downstairs.

"Just like this?"

"When it's just you. I mean, you always look beautiful no matter what you do with yourself, but right now, you are exquisite."

"My hair is damp, I have no makeup on, and I'm wearing my most comfortable clothing aside from pajamas," I said.

"Exactly."

"You started a fire," I said.

"I did," he said.

When I joined him next to it, he wrapped his arm around me. His skin felt warmer from standing next to the flames.

"It's made you feel warm," I said.

"I thought you'd like that for a change."

"I love you the way you are," I said.

"As I do you," Azriel said and kissed the top of my head gently.

"What about when I'm old and gray, and you're still young?"

"That will never happen," he said.

"What do you mean?"

Azriel turned me to face him. "You're already going to age very slowly because of your witch blood. Look at your mother and your Aunties. But you've also got my blood coursing through your veins now."

"But you said I'm not a vampire."

"You're not, Kinsley. Not fully, but you will age very, very slowly. When you get to the point you don't want to age at all anymore, I can turn you completely. We can be together forever," he said and kissed my forehead before softly pressing his lips to mine.

"What if I decide I don't want to be a vampire?" I asked.

"Then you will find a way to turn me human and I'll grow old and die with you."

"You'd do that?" I asked.

"There would be no point in being on this Earth anymore if you're not here with me," he said.

"I bet you say that to all the girls."

"When I told you that I had never loved anyone before, I meant that."

"What about Tangerine?" I asked, suddenly feeling the need to lighten the conversation. "Where is she anyway?"

"I was riding too hard to get to you to bring her along," Azriel said. "I've got some buddies heading this way in a few days. Once I give the word that I'm staying, they'll bring her here."

"Are you?" I asked.

"Am I staying?"

"Yeah, are you staying here this time?"

"Kinsley, I think that's up to you," he said.

"I want you to stay, Azriel. Stay here with me."

"On one condition," he said, and the burning look in his eyes took my breath away.

"What's that?"

"You be my wife."

"I, uh… Are you going to bring the whole gang back to the old Coke plant and everything?"

"I can't tell if that's a yes or if you're saying my crew is a part of the deal," Azriel said with a chuckle. "It would just be me. I'd have to get a job."

"You'd do that for me?"

"Well, I was actually thinking of opening a shop."

"Like a gift shop?" I was a little confused by all that was going on.

"Like a bike shop, Kinsley. I would do special orders and custom builds. I've got a lot of connections in the industry."

"You might end up in one of those reality TV shows," I said. "They haven't had a good biker one for a while."

"No," Azriel said.

"Yes."

"Seriously, Kinsley. I'm not doing reality TV."

"No, I mean yes. I'll be your wife. I can't imagine ever being without you again."

"Did you just decide that right now?" Azriel asked.

"Well, I mean… you did just ask me to be your wife. So, yes?"

"I mean the part about you never wanting to be without me again. Did you just decide that right now?"

"If I did, does that mean you're withdrawing your proposal?"

"No, Kinsley. The fact that you decided it at all is good enough for me," he said. "So, when do we do this? When do we seal the deal?"

"That was a really romantic way of putting it," I said with a laugh.

"I try to be a gentleman, baby, but there's still a whole lot of biker in me."

"I can deal with it," I said with a teasing eye roll. "I mean, we could call Lilith back and do a handfasting tonight. There's a waxing moon. It's the perfect time for it. We don't have any rings or anything, but that's okay."

"I have a ring," he said and pulled a little black velvet box out of his pocket.

He opened it and showed me a platinum band with three diamonds. The center diamond was a round cut, and on each side were diamonds cut in the shape of the crescent moon representing the full lunar cycle.

"Oh my gosh," I said.

"I had it made for you."

"How did you know I'd say yes? That thing must have cost a fortune."

"I took a chance," he said. "So, why don't you call Lilith and ask her to come back. I'll pour the wine."

"I was just kidding, but okay," I said and took a deep breath. "Can you make margaritas instead?"

"Margaritas?" he asked.

"It's a thing," I said. "I'll show you the movie sometime."

"Okay, I'll make margaritas."

"I'll call Lilith, but we don't have a ring for you. That's okay, though. We don't have to have rings for a handfasting."

"I have a ring for me," Azriel said with a smile. "The rings are a set. I had one made for me too."

And just like that, my parents, Amelda, and Lilith, as well as any other Aunties they could reach, came back to our house. Viv and Reggie were already in bed, but they threw on some clothes and rushed back over to my house.

I married Azriel under the light of a nearly full waxing moon. It was like eloping impetuously, but your whole family was there cheering you on.

At least with my family, doing something so nuts was completely encouraged. Almost murdered and married in the same day.

I had to wonder what the future had in store for me.

Chapter Eleven

I met with Thorn the next day to give him my statement about finding Dante's body. I sat in my car for ten minutes before going into the station, debating about whether to wear the ring or not. I turned it around and around on my finger, and I wouldn't realize until later that I was turning it counterclockwise.

In the end, I decided to wear it. He was going to find out eventually. If he hadn't heard already, it would only be a matter of hours.

I took the knife with me too. The one Dante had used to stab me. Thorn didn't know what had happened, and it wasn't like he could write an official report about it, but it still felt like I should at least explain what had happened.

He stared at my ring the entire time I was talking. I watched as he would only write down the parts of my statement could go in the official record.

"Are you okay?" he asked me when I finally finished the story.

"I am," I said. "I'm okay now."

"You're engaged to him, then?" Thorn's voice was strained, and I could tell he was trying to hold back emotion.

I don't know what it was about that, but it hurt my heart. I was supposed to be happy, but I would be fine once I got home and back to my new husband.

"Married," I said. "We did a handfasting last night."

"So, not legally married."

"I don't know why you felt like you had to point that out, but I'm going to let it go," I said as gently as I could. "How is it going with your new lady friend?" I asked, not because I wanted to know but because I wanted to point out that he had someone else as well. It wasn't just me. I wasn't the only one who had torn us apart.

"It's not," he said through a tight semi-smile. "I would have talked to you about that, but there's no point now." He took a deep breath and straightened his back. "What I do want to ask you about is Detective Devereaux."

"What about him?" I asked after swallowing the lump in my throat.

"Did he ever say anything or do anything that made you uncomfortable? I don't know… Did he ever say anything or do anything that might have made you think he was… involved?"

"In the murder?" I asked.

"Yeah," Thorn said.

"Not really. He was following us around, I guess. I didn't think that was that unusual. Why do you ask?"

"I don't know, Kinsley. The guy rubbed me the wrong way, so I started looking into him. He's had a lot of problems with the department. Stuff that would have gotten him fired before Hurricane Lara and all of the police union changes that came along with it in Louisiana. A big part of me has to wonder if his chief let him come here because he wanted him out of his hair."

"And you think he might have followed Liberty down here and killed her?" I asked.

"Well, he said she stole something but that he couldn't disclose what it was. Apparently, there's an ongoing case with him where he's being investigated by Internal Affairs for possibly taking evidence. Cash. They've searched his house, and no one has ever found any trace of the money."

"So, you think she might have stolen it? That would explain why he wanted to know so badly everywhere she'd been in Coventry. Maybe he thinks she hid the money here."

"Stay away from him, okay? If you have to talk to him, do it in public. If he asks to meet with you, do it here at the station."

"Okay," I said. "Is there anything else?"

"No. Nothing right now. Take care of yourself, Kinsley."

As I was leaving, I tried not to think about what Thorn had said about there not being another woman in his life. How he was going to talk to me about it, but there was no longer any point.

It didn't matter anymore though… He was right about that. I just needed to get back to my new husband so we could have breakfast together. I'd make some bacon and eggs before I headed into my store for the day.

Azriel had mentioned something about going to look for space for his shop, so I wasn't that shocked that his bike was gone from the driveway. He'd retrieved it the night before when I was getting ready for bed, but I figured he must have wanted to get an early start on looking for a space to rent. It was a good thing he was eager. We had a life to begin together.

Shortly after I pulled into the driveway, Suki and Rosie appeared from across the street. She must have taken Suki for a walk in the cemetery.

"Hey, guys!" I said and waved at them.

Suki walked Rosie over to the edge of my driveway. "Good morning, Kinsley. How are you today?"

"I'm doing well. How are you, Suki? How are your magical workings going?"

"Oh, so much better. So, so much better. It's like I was blocked before, and now the energy of the universe is just flowing through me," she said.

"That's amazing," I said. "I'm happy for you. It's always great when a witch comes into her powers."

"It is," Suki agreed.

I knelt so I could give Rosie a thorough petting and a complete skritching. As I was scratching around her neck under her collar, something stuck to my finger.

When I pulled my hand away, there was a tiny, heart-shaped picture stuck to my fingers. Suki was looking off in the other direction, so she didn't see it. I shoved the little picture into my pocket and stood up.

"Well, I better be going. My mother and father are here for breakfast, and I've got to get into the shop later," I said.

"Have a good day, Kinsley," Suki said in a voice that sounded almost sing-songy.

I could swear something dark flashed in her eyes, but I just hurried into the house. I looked at the picture while I was trying to call Thorn. It was a picture of Jeremy, Reggie's boyfriend.

Why would a locket with Jeremy's picture have been near the crime scene? And how did the picture from it end up stuck to Rosie's collar? Did Suki and Lottie know each other?

A loud thud against the side of my house startled me. It was quickly followed by another one, but that time, whatever it was hit my front window. I heard the glass crack, but the house didn't let it break.

Meri came skittering down the stairs. "What was that?"

"I don't know," I said. "I'm trying to call Thorn because..." Another loud thud. "Never mind, I'll tell you later. Anyway, I can't get ahold of him because it's going right to voicemail. Any idea where Azriel is?"

Another thud against the glass.

"He was looking through stuff, and then he said, *later, cat,* and left," Meri said.

"Looking through stuff? Did he go into the attic?"

"No, I hid that from him," Meri said proudly.

"Okay. Well, what was he going through?"

Whatever was hitting the house hit the front door.

"Just everything but the attic. Basement, cabinets, dresser drawers. Anyway, we can worry about that later, can't we?"

"Yeah. You're right. I'm going to see what's going on."

I went to the front window and peeled back the curtain. Suki was standing just off my porch throwing fist-sized rocks at my house. The landscaping beds in the front of the house were lined with gray river rocks dotted with the occasional geode. She was picking them up and winging them at the house.

"That's a new one," I said as Meri jumped into the window to see.

"I'll take care of it," Meri said.

"No, I'll do it," I retorted.

"We'll just do it together."

"Fine. Yeah. Let's go," I said.

I went out the front door, and Suki had moved to the bottom of the front steps. Before I could get my bearings, she winged a rock at me and hit me right in the temple.

Stars exploded in front of my eyes, and I went down to one knee. Fortunately, it was just a rock, and I was able to heal myself before I went unconscious.

"Damn you and your stupid healing powers," Suki spat at me. "I wish I could bind you the way she bound me!"

I felt a slight prick as the tiny bit of magic she could control tried to bind me, but Suki was no match for me. She wasn't even any match for Meri.

He ran over and circled her legs before rubbing against them. When he did, she collapsed on the ground and sat cross-legged and docile. Meri had rendered her unable to move.

I'd left a message on Thorn's voicemail, so I knew he'd come eventually. While I had her captive there, I figured I'd get the truth out of Suki.

"Speak," I said and snapped my fingers. It was then that I saw Rosie cowering and shaking over by the hangman's tree. "Rosie, go lie down." I pointed to the porch.

She obeyed and ran up my porch steps. When Rosie lay down at the top of the steps to keep an eye on what was happening, Meri curled up next to her. She gave him a big lick on the top of the head. Meri rolled his eyes, but I was glad he was able to calm her.

"Back to you," I said to Suki. "Speak."

"He was mine," Suki spat at me.

"Who was yours?"

"Jeremy."

So, it turned out that Lottie wasn't the only woman obsessed with Jeremy. Suki had also been in love with Jeremy, but in her case, it was from a distance.

She'd even tried to use a love potion on him, but that had backfired. Love potions were always a bad idea because they interfered with another person's free will. You couldn't make someone love you, and in some cases, there were dire consequences when you tried.

In Suki's case, her spell just made Jeremy completely ignore her. That didn't make Suki give up, though. It only deepened her obsessive need to make Jeremy fall in love with her.

Suki hated Reggie for being with Jeremy, but she also hated Liberty for helping Lottie. Apparently, Suki tried to hire Liberty as well, but the Voodoo priestess turned her down. Suki was too unhinged.

"That's what she said to me. She said I was unhinged, and I needed therapy, not help from the spirits," Suki said when she got to that point in the story.

"I think she might have been right," I said.

Apparently, Suki frightened Liberty so much that she bound her magic. Liberty had no idea that Suki would kill her for it. She never should have come back to Coventry, but the allure of how much money she could make playing Lottie off me was too tempting. That, and she was apparently running from trouble down in New Orleans.

Unfortunately, killing Liberty didn't unbind Suki. She'd tied the binding to her husband. So, he had to die too.

"But why did he try to kill me?" I asked. "Did he really still think I'd killed Liberty?"

"I have no idea why he tried to kill you," Suki said. "It had nothing to do with me."

"She's confessed to killing Liberty and Dante," I said to Thorn as one of his deputies put Suki in the back of a cruiser. "She'll confess to you too."

"Thank you," Thorn said. "Are you sure you're okay?"

He was asking me that a lot suddenly.

"Yeah. Um… I'm not sure."

"Not sure about what?" Thorn asked.

"Oh, it's just that when I got back, Azriel was gone. Meri said he was going through stuff, and then he just took off. I think maybe he's visiting potential places to open his custom motorcycle shop. I'm sure he left a note or something inside," I said and shook my head as if I could just shake away the bad feeling creeping into my chest.

"Kinsley."

"It's okay," I said. "I'm sure it's fine, Thorn. Besides, you're the last person I should be dumping this on. Not that there's anything to dump."

"I'm here anytime you need me," he said earnestly.

"Thanks," I said through a tight smile.

Chapter Twelve

There was no note, and Azriel wouldn't answer his phone or texts. Two days later when he still hadn't come home, I had to admit that he probably wasn't out looking for places to rent for his bike shop.

Another day went by, and before I left for work that morning, Thorn turned up on my doorstep. "I need to talk to you."

"What is it?" The gravity in his voice made my heart thunder like it was going to punch its way out of my chest. "Is it Azriel?"

"Can I come in? I'd like for us to sit down and talk."

I swallowed another huge lump in my throat. The feeling that something had happened to Azriel was irrational. He was a vampire, after all. It wasn't like he was going to get in a car accident and die or something.

"Sure, come in. Would you like coffee?"

"We need to talk first," Thorn said.

"It's already made," I insisted. "Won't take me but a minute to pour you a cup."

"Okay, Kinsley," he said softly. "Sure, please. I'll have a cup."

I busied myself for a couple of minutes fixing his cup of coffee the way he liked. I knew I really didn't want to hear what he had to say.

Finally, I had to set the cup down in front of him and plant my butt in a chair as well. My legs wouldn't stop moving, though. My fingers drummed the table with anxiety.

"What happened to him?" I asked.

"I don't know," Thorn said.

"Wait, what? Why are you here then?"

"I'm here about the knife you gave me the day you came in and gave your statement. I need to know something, Kinsley. After he saved you, did Azriel ever touch the knife?"

"I don't think so," I said. "He was going to leave it there, but I picked it up. I insisted on bringing it home. Why?"

"I dusted it for prints and ran what I found, Kinsley. Your prints were on it and Dante's too. That wasn't unexpected. When I found the third set of prints, well that was a mystery. Until I ran them."

"No," I said, and I felt the room start to swirl around me.

"They were Azriel's. I found them in an FBI database. One that I'm not supposed to have access too, but I'm glad that I do."

I keeled halfway over and almost fell out of my chair. Fortunately, Thorn caught me.

It didn't all make sense just yet, and I hadn't put all of the pieces together, but I knew it was true. I remembered the offhand comment Azriel made about him being a vampire and knowing things about New Orleans.

"I'm so sorry," I said as I slid the ring off my finger and put it down on the kitchen table.

I finally took a good look at it. In the soft light of the fire or outside under the moon, it had looked beautiful, but inside under the harsher lights of my kitchen, it became obvious that it was just a cheap piece of costume jewelry. I'd willfully ignored the truth about it and about Azriel too.

"I'm sorry, Thorn."

"There's no need for that," he said and put his hand over the top of mine. "Not right now, anyway."

"But, I…"

"Kinsley, we both played a role in this. I wasn't exactly a saint."

"Did something actually happen between you and the other woman?" I asked, but I wasn't sure why. It's not like I really wanted to know if it had. "You might as well tell me now."

"Nothing," he said. "I didn't even end up asking her out. I was going to tell you about her the other day when you came in to give your statement, but you'd already married Azriel. I didn't see a point in bringing it up then, but I'll tell you now if you want."

"Sure," I said, knowing that it would make him stay a little longer. I wasn't ready for him to leave me alone with the information he'd delivered.

"It's not super sordid or complicated. I was feeling jealous of what had happened between you and Azriel, and I invested myself emotionally in the first woman who was nice to me. Well, not just nice to me, but someone who I might have asked out before you."

"I didn't think you dated much before me."

"I didn't, but there were women I considered asking out occasionally. Of course, when I turned my attention to Aimee, that's her name in case you're wondering, I was just hurting. I hate to compare women, but compared to you, she'd never really make me happy. No woman could stand up to you. Probably never will again."

"Oh, Thorn," I said and felt tears well up.

"It's okay, Kinsley," he said and squeezed my hand again. "I know now is not the time, but I want you to know that I'll fight too."

"You still… after all this?" I felt my chest contract.

"I'll always love you, Kinsley. It's why it was so hard for me to say it at first and why it took me too long. Because it's not something that I would just throw around. It's for life."

"I'm sorry that I threw us away for whatever that was with Azriel," I said. "It wasn't even real. He was just manipulating me, and I fell for it a second time."

"You may be the most powerful witch in the world, but Kinsley, you're still vulnerable. He was a predator with a different kind of magic. You know from the way the Voodoo worked that there are things out there that can hurt you."

"I wish I could go back. I wish I could take it all back."

"You can't, though," Thorn said. "But that doesn't mean we can't go forward."

"You still want to be with me after all this?" I couldn't believe it.

"I do, Kinsley," he said and rubbed my back gently. "But it's not the time for that right now. You need some time to heal. You know that there will never be anybody for me but you, so we don't have to rush back into things. Why don't we try friends for now? Why don't we try being friends who don't yell at each other or do things to hurt one another, and let nature take its course from there?"

"So, we're even then?" I said with my first smile in two days.

"Yeah, we can say that. I still have a lot to make up to you."

"You have a lot to make up to me? Thorn, I married another man."

"Yeah, but it wasn't legal," he said with a wink, and that made me laugh. "And I can't help feel like I neglected you during our relationship. I pushed you into his arms, and I accept my responsibility in that. If I had been there for you the way you were there for me, then I don't think any of this would have happened."

"Thorn…"

"What would you like to eat?" he said and stood up from the table. "I'm not the best in the kitchen, but I think I can manage a mean grilled cheese."

"You don't have to cook for me," I said.

"I know I don't have to, but Kinsley, when was the last time you had a good meal?"

"Is it that obvious?" I hadn't been eating much the last couple of days.

"Yeah, honey, it is."

"There's tomato soup in the pantry too. I like to dip the grilled cheese."

"I know," he said and headed for the pantry.

"I can help," I said.

"You can supervise," Thorn said. "Make sure I don't burn the kitchen down, okay? I don't know what the future is going to bring, Kinsley, or exactly how we're going to work through this, but for tonight, just let me take care of you."

"Okay."

"Is he going to make me bacon?" Meri said as sauntered into the room. "I let you guys have your little chat about super-serious human things, but I'm hungry."

"And bacon for the cat," Thorn said with a smile. "Do you want two or four slices?"

"Six."

"Meri," I said.

"Six," he insisted.

"Okay, fine. Let him have six."

"Thanks, creature," he said and jumped into my lap.

"You're welcome," I said and patted his head.

"Whatever."

Epilogue

Three Weeks Later

My eyes shot open, and I sat up in bed. The last time a stomach cramp like that woke me up, I was a kid. Stomach flu had hit Coventry hard that winter, but I only had to deal with it for a half an hour or so before my mom found me worshiping the porcelain goddess in the guest bathroom and healed me.

As I ran for the commode, something told me I didn't have the stomach flu. I'd already begun to suspect something wasn't quite right with me. There'd been a shift in my energy away from me, but also still within me. I'd told myself my magic was just maturing.

Ha.

Meri just stared at me as I brushed my teeth.

"You feeling okay?" he asked when I was done.

"We were only married for one day," I said, still swimming in my river of denial.

"I'm no expert, but I hear that's all it takes," Meri said not nearly as smugly as I expected.

"I can't be," I said and brushed my hair as if it could change the wheel of fate.

"I mean, you could be. You've met all of the requisite conditions," Meri said. "Hey, I'm hungry. If you're feeling up to it, I'd like my breakfast."

"I'm hungry too," I said.

"You just spent like fifteen minutes heaving into the commode."

"And now I'm starving."

"Oh, no," Meri said. "We're in trouble."

"What do you mean?" I asked as I swam farther away from the banks and into the deep end of denial.

"I do not want another creature," Meri huffed. "All I want is some bacon."

Thank you for reading!

Grab the next book in the series:

Book of Dark Magic

Made in the USA
Columbia, SC
28 November 2020

25752839R00126